Crosspatch

A Southern Quilting Mystery, Volume 17

Elizabeth Craig

Published by Elizabeth Spann Craig, 2022.

This is a work of fiction. Similarities to real people, places, or events are entirely coincidental.

CROSSPATCH

First edition. October 4, 2022.

Copyright © 2022 Elizabeth Craig.

Written by Elizabeth Craig.

Chapter One

It had been a lovely church service so far. Beatrice was sitting on one of the old wooden pews. Light was cheerfully streaming through the stained glass, throwing various colorful hues over the members of the congregation. The organist's music had complemented the choir perfectly, and the hymns were stirring.

But then Ace Lincoln's cell phone went off in the middle of Wyatt's thoughtful and meaningful pastoral prayer. And Beatrice's teeth were suddenly on edge.

It wasn't the first time Ace's phone had gone off in the middle of the service. Actually, it had happened every week for the last month. It seemed to be set at an earthshaking volume and appeared to be programmed to go off during Wyatt's prayer each week—the quietest part of the service. Plus, the phone's ringtone was *Joyful, Joyful, We Adore Thee*, which only served to make Beatrice feel rather guilty at her irritation over the disruption.

Ace gave everyone a sheepish grin and strode out the door, phone still warbling its hymn. Even worse, Ace started talking to the caller before he'd even gotten all the way out of the sanctuary. It was most disturbing.

Beatrice's daughter, Piper, who was seated next to her, gave her a wink before they resumed praying. She'd heard her mother talk about Ace before and bemoaning the fact that his phone never seemed to be on silent mode.

Thankfully, the rest of the service was just as lovely as the first bit. And when Ace did return to the sanctuary, his phone didn't make another peep.

As soon as church was over, Piper said teasingly, "Mama, you did a good job keeping yourself under control. You only turned a little red that time."

Beatrice sighed. "There are just a few things that really punch my buttons. Anyway, it was a lovely service. Would y'all like to have Sunday dinner with us?"

Ash, Piper's husband, said, "Oh, we don't want to make you have to cook today."

"It's no problem at all," said Beatrice with a grin. "Madelyn Templeton came by yesterday with a chicken casserole, biscuits, and green beans almondine. It's a huge casserole, intended to feed six or eight people. Besides, Meadow and Ramsay will be there."

"That was awfully nice of Madelyn. Do y'all often get great meals? I might have to drop by more often," she said teasingly.

"All the time. People can be very thoughtful." Beatrice realized her annoyance at people who were *not* thoughtful was greatly diminished when she dwelled on the people who *were*.

Piper said, "Then we'd love to come. Ash and I will collect Will from the nursery and meet you over there."

Beatrice smiled at her. "Just let yourself in if you get there before we do. I've got to collect *Wyatt*, which can be a longer task."

As it happened, though, getting away from the church was a fairly speedy process this time. The members of the congregation very quickly told Wyatt he'd delivered a good sermon, and then they all hurried off to their own Sunday dinners with family. Wyatt smiled at Beatrice as they walked home. "Were you able to get Piper and Ash to join us?"

Beatrice nodded. "They're picking up Will and will meet us there."

He reached out for her hand and she gave his a squeeze. It was an absolutely beautiful day with a strikingly blue sky. A gentle breeze blew around them as they made the short walk home.

Piper, Ash, and Will had indeed beaten them to the house, despite Wyatt's relatively quick exit. Noo-noo, their corgi, was apparently delighted with the surprise visit and was "helping" Ash and Will play with plastic blocks on the floor as Piper heated up the sides in the microwave and had the casserole in the oven to reheat. Wyatt started setting the table and Beatrice went into the kitchen to give Piper a hand.

"It smells wonderful," said Beatrice.

"Well, I spent all night cooking it," said Piper with a wink. "I'll take credit for it, even though all I've done is heat it up. How was the past week, Mama?"

"Pretty good, I guess. I've felt like all I've really done lately is to be sedentary, though. I truly *love* being sedentary and just reading a book or working on a quilt, but I think the inactivity is starting to catch up with me. For some reason, the longer I sit, the longer I *want* to sit. I haven't even made trips to the church for the Pilates class. On the upside, I've gotten some good quilting done, including some work on my UFO." Beatrice gave Piper a mischievous look.

The quilt guild had a UFO or unfinished objects swap as their activity last month. The members were to hand over a quilt they'd quit working on to another guild member and let them complete it. Beatrice had one of Piper's.

Piper gave her mother a wry look. "Thanks for reminding me. I still have a lot of work to do on my UFO before the meeting."

"It's not as if you have a lot of free time to quilt," said Beatrice sympathetically. "It must be hard to carve out some time for yourself these days." Between Will, Piper's part-time job, and keeping up with things at home, Beatrice knew Piper's plate was full.

"Oh, I squeeze a few moments in here and there. Quilting is very relaxing for me, so it's worth it. And Will *does* take naps, so that helps."

Beatrice raised an eyebrow. "I thought they always say moms are supposed to take naps when their babies do."

Piper snorted. "They do say that, but I think these experts have never had babies before. Naptime's when I scamper around trying to catch up. But I'll admit I leave the last ten minutes of naptime for me to put my feet up."

"How do you know you have ten minutes? Are Will's naptimes that predictable?"

Piper said, "Oh, I just wait until I hear him stirring over the baby monitor. I know at that point I'll have ten minutes of him gradually waking up before he starts to fuss and call for me. But going back to what we were talking about—do you really feel like you've been sedentary? You've always been so active. In fact, I always felt like you've had a hard time sitting still."

"That's usually the case, but it hasn't been lately. I'll have to take Noo-noo out for a longer walk today."

The little corgi, who'd been avidly watching to see if any food fell to the floor, perked up as she heard the magic word *walk*. Her gaze drifted over to her harness hanging by the front door.

Piper asked, "Does walking Noo-noo help you with exercise? I thought she was forever stopping to smell interesting scents on the side of the road."

Noo-noo gave Piper a reproachful look.

Beatrice sighed. "You're right, it probably isn't enough exercise, especially considering how inactive I've been. I've been meaning to get out and work in the yard, too, but the weather hasn't been too conducive to that lately. And, with all the rain we've had, the weeds are out of control."

Piper said, "I was thinking more of a real exercise class instead of yardwork."

Beatrice frowned. "An exercise class? Isn't that like going from zero to sixty in a few seconds?"

"For some of the classes, maybe. But this is a beginner's class. The instructor is Summer Cooper, and she's supposed to be really good. She taught classes in Lenoir for a long time and then decided to open her own studio here in Dappled Hills. She teaches both group classes and individual."

Wyatt had walked into the kitchen to fill everyone's glasses with water, overheard their conversation, and noticed Beatrice was still looking unsure. He said, "Are you planning on going to one of the classes, Piper?"

She nodded. "I'm going to give it a go tomorrow. Ash is going to head to work a little later than usual and can watch Will while I go to the class. I'd love if you tried it out with me, Mama. I'm allowed to bring a guest with me."

Beatrice smiled at her. "For you? Of course. But I have a feeling I'll be moving at a much slower pace than everyone else. Where is her studio? I haven't noticed any new construction lately."

"It's actually right behind the house where Summer and her husband live. You probably know Harlowe—he's the manager at Bub's Grocery. Anyway, they have a big lot and Summer thought it would be very convenient if she could just slip back into the back and work there. She just had the place built, and it's finally finished."

Beatrice said, "And there's enough parking? Even for a group class?"

Piper nodded. "That's what she said, anyway. Apparently, they have over an acre and her husband developed some of it into a gravel lot for parking."

Beatrice said, "I'll meet you over there, then, Piper. I have to say I'm curious. Plus, I'm getting a little tired of my own exercise routine. Maybe I need some new ideas."

Piper glanced at her watch. "I thought you said Meadow and Ramsay were joining us."

Ash glanced over from the living room. "Mom planned on coming over. And when I called her when we arrived to let her know Piper and I were going to be here, she was especially excited. You know she never misses the chance to see Will."

Beatrice frowned. "That's true. Maybe we should give them a call. It's not like them to run late and they're only just down the street."

Which was right when Beatrice's door flew open and Meadow, breathless, appeared. "Mercy! I was starting to think I wouldn't get here at all."

Ash stood up and walked over. "Did something happen? And where's Dad?"

Meadow plopped down in a chair around the dining room table. "Boris created a bit of drama, that's all."

Boris was Meadow and Ramsay's large dog of somewhat indeterminate heritage. He could be a handful, but he had such an engaging doggy smile that it was tempting to forgive him for any misbehavior.

Wyatt put a glass of water in front of her. "Dog shenanigans?" he asked.

Meadow nodded. "I'll say. When Ramsay and I got home from church, we discovered Boris had somehow gotten up on the high counter and had eaten *all* the biscuits from a zipper bag I'd planned on bringing over."

Beatrice had to admit to feeling sad about the devoured biscuits. Meadow was quite the cook. She had the feeling the canned biscuits she'd stuck in the oven weren't quite the same.

Piper frowned. "Is Boris okay? That sounds like a lot of bread to have eaten."

"And did he eat any of the zipper bag?" asked Ash.

Meadow wagged a finger at him. "That's exactly what the vet wanted to know. But somehow, he got the biscuits out without eating any of the plastic. I was planning on running him over to the vet, but then he had a terrible bout of indigestion and emptied his tummy of most of the food."

Beatrice grimaced. "Charming."

"I know. Then Ramsay helped me clean it all up. We thought Ramsay better stay home and keep an eye on Boris, so the last I saw them, they were curled up together taking a nap."

Piper said, "Well, tell him we missed him."

They filled their plates with food, Wyatt blessed it, and they dug in. Meadow was charmed the whole time by Will's new ability to handle a fork. "Look at him! He's brilliant."

Although Beatrice found herself disagreeing with Meadow on many things, she had to agree she was right about their mutual grandson. Will beamed at the praise and then promptly dropped the fork on the floor, which made them all chuckle as Ash got up to find him another fork.

Piper said, "Meadow, Mama and I just made plans to go to Summer's new exercise studio tomorrow morning. Want to join us?"

"No, thank you! I'm not sure group exercise is exactly my cup of tea. Besides, I wouldn't have anything to wear."

Piper said, "Oh, you don't have to worry about wearing fancy exercise clothes. I'm planning on just wearing a pair of capri pants and a tee shirt."

Beatrice said wryly, "I'm likely wearing my Pilates outfit since I don't really have anything else."

Meadow made a face. "I can see my usual excuse isn't going to work with you two, so now I have to get real. I intensely dislike exercising."

Piper looked surprised. "Do you? You always seem to enjoy your walks with Boris."

"Walking with Boris is not necessarily exercise unless Boris starts sprinting after a rabbit."

Beatrice helpfully pointed out, "You also do a lot of gardening."

"Yes, but that's because I like the outcome. If I weren't getting tomatoes and summer squash out of the transaction, I certainly wouldn't be out there working in the garden. No, I'm afraid I'm going to have to leave you two with it." Meadow's voice didn't sound very sorry at all, actually.

Ash grinned at his mother. "Maybe you should give it a go. It could be fun exercising with Piper and Beatrice."

"You're not helping, Ash! Of *course* it would be *more* pleasurable with Piper and Beatrice, but the enjoyment I'd take in their company would not be enough to put up with the exercising portion of the outing."

Meadow was looking quite huffy now and Wyatt, always the peacemaker, quickly stepped in. "I'd say you lead a pretty active life, Meadow."

She gave him a tremendous smile. "Thank you! Indeed, I do. As do you, I think. Catch us up with everything going on at the church."

Wyatt gave a little wrap-up of upcoming events as Will, ever-mindful of what generates the best response, theatrically threw his fork on the floor again. This time, there was no replacement fork, but since Will was now eating Cheerio cereal, none was really required. Beatrice was enjoying herself so much that she ate a bit more than she'd intended. She reflected later that afternoon that it was indeed good she'd be exercising the next morning.

Chapter Two

Despite her eagerness to work off the Sunday lunch, by the next morning Beatrice felt less like exercising. The sun was just a faint orb in the sky, obscured by dark clouds that hinted at rain or drizzle at the very least. She wanted nothing more than to stay in her well-worn robe and slippers and read her book while curled up with Noo-noo on the sofa. Instead, she dragged herself into her exercise clothes and hurried out to her car to meet Piper.

Summer's house and studio were in a heavily wooded area not too far away. Beatrice pulled into the gravel parking lot, avoiding a large tree that must have fallen during the storm the night before. She glanced around her. Piper hadn't come yet and Beatrice had no desire to go in and chat with Summer, who she didn't know, before Piper arrived. Instead, she leaned back in her driver's seat and closed her eyes briefly. She realized she should have had a bit more coffee before attempting to exercise.

At some point, she must have fallen asleep because she was startled by a light tapping on her window. Piper looked through the glass at her sympathetically. Beatrice quickly gathered her keys, phone, and small purse and opened the car door. "Sorry. I must have drifted off." She stifled a yawn.

"Sorry I'm a little late. Everything seemed to be conspiring against me this morning," said Piper. "Will had gotten food all over himself and I was trying to clean him up while Ash got ready for work so he could just leave when I got home."

"Doesn't Will normally like baths?" asked Beatrice.

Piper made a face. "Not this morning, unfortunately. He started crying and then couldn't seem to *stop* crying. He was really wailing when I left. I felt sorry for Ash."

"But you deserve some time to yourself, too," said Beatrice. "Exercise will give you more energy for handling Will the rest of the day."

"That's what Ash said, too. Anyway, I'm glad we planned on meeting up this morning because I already feel exhausted. I probably wouldn't have even made it here if we hadn't decided to come together." She glanced across at her mother. "Hey, I like your exercise clothes! Are those new?"

Beatrice grinned at her. "New to me. I actually saw them hanging in the window of the consignment shop. They still had their tags on them."

"You keep finding these amazing things at the consignment shop. Every time I go in there, it seems like they don't have anything that cute."

Beatrice said, "The trick is to go in there frequently. Since it's right near the Patchwork Cottage, I just stick my head in for a few minutes before I shop for fabric. The problem is, you don't have a lot of extra time. How about if I keep an eye out for goodies for you . . . and for Will."

"Since you're the one with the good luck there, that would be awesome! Especially for Will. He's been growing like a weed."

Beatrice and Piper followed a sign from the parking lot toward the studio.

"No one else is here yet?" asked Beatrice, frowning.

"I guess not. That tells me Summer hasn't done a good job getting the word out. Maybe she needs to do some advertising or something."

"Or it tells us that this is perhaps a little early for an exercise class," murmured Beatrice.

Piper grinned at her. "Did you not get much sleep last night?"

"It's weird, but it was like all sounds and lights were extra-amplified. I could hear Noo-noo snoring, and she wasn't even in the same room with us. Then I suppose she got restless later on and I kept hearing her little toenails tapping on the hard-wood floor. And of course we had a huge storm last night and I couldn't sleep during it. I guess sleep just wasn't on the agenda for me last night. Did you get any?"

"Slept like a dream last night, actually. Storm or no storm."

Beatrice made a face. "It says something about my sleeping when my daughter, who has a baby, is sleeping better than I am."

"Well, after we exercise this morning, I bet you'll sleep great tonight."

They walked up to the studio behind the large house. The studio was bigger than Beatrice thought it would be—a one-story building that was brightly lit from the inside. There were flower boxes in the windows and landscaping around it. Beatrice was already impressed, and they hadn't even made it inside yet.

"I guess we just walk right in," said Piper, sounding a little hesitant. It did feel almost as if they were walking into some-one's house.

Piper opened the door, and they walked in. She called out, "Summer? It's Piper. I've brought my mom with me as a guest."

There was no response. They were standing in a small coatroom with lots of hooks for hanging sweaters, raincoats, or umbrellas.

"Maybe she has earbuds in and is warming up," suggested Beatrice.

Piper said, "Or maybe she's still doing some last-minute tweaks to the studio." She called Summer's name again, but they heard nothing.

Beatrice and Piper headed for the large room on the other side of the coatroom. It was clearly the main studio, with equipment lining the walls and mirrors everywhere. And, most surprisingly, the body of a blonde woman in the center of the floor.

Chapter Three

Piper took a deep, gasping breath. "Oh no."

Beatrice carefully approached the woman, who was lying on her stomach on the floor. With a shaking hand, she felt for a pulse. There wasn't one.

"I'm afraid she's gone," said Beatrice grimly.

Piper pulled her phone out and started dialing Ramsay's number. Ramsay was the local police chief and Beatrice's friend, Meadow's, husband.

While Piper quietly reported the crime, Beatrice glanced around the brand-new studio. It looked as if Summer had been hit from behind with the hot-pink ten-pound hand weight that was next to her.

Piper ended the conversation and said, "Mama, Ramsay asked if we could wait for him outside the studio."

They quickly moved outside without touching anything but the doorknob, which they used a tissue to grip.

It didn't take long before Ramsay's police sedan pulled into the gravel parking lot. Ramsay, a big man with a receding hairline, hurried toward them. He greeted them gruffly, sounding a bit as if he might have just woken up. Then he proceeded cautiously into the studio. A minute later, he came back outside and started stringing up police tape.

"Do either of you know who the woman inside is?" he asked in a somber voice.

Piper nodded. "It's Summer Cooper. She owns the studio."

Ramsay nodded, taking out a small notepad and an even smaller stub of a pencil. He looked at the large home behind them. "Is that her residence?"

Piper cleared her throat. "It is. She lives there with her husband, Harlowe."

"I'm sorry you two had to come across her this way. Can you fill me in a little as to who Summer is and what your morning looked like so far?"

So Piper did. "Summer used to teach classes in Lenoir for another place, but then she decided to open her own studio. This was actually her grand opening." Piper swallowed, thinking of it. "I got a free trial and asked Mama if she wanted to try out a group class with me."

Ramsay raised his eyebrows. "A group class? Where is everyone else?"

Beatrice said, "Piper and I were just talking about that before we walked in and saw Summer. Piper was saying Summer needed to advertise some more."

Ramsay continued, "So the two of you walked into the studio and what did you see?"

"We were a little surprised that Summer didn't come right out and greet us," said Piper slowly. "We thought maybe she had her earbuds in and was warming up or getting ready for the class or something."

"We put our bags down and walked in and saw Summer on the floor—exactly as we left her," said Beatrice. "I checked for a pulse but, aside from that, we didn't touch anything."

"You did great," said Ramsay in a gentle voice.

They heard someone call down to them from outside the house.

Ramsay said in a grim voice, "Is that Harlowe? Summer's husband?"

"I'm afraid so," answered Piper.

Harlowe was a tall, thin man, handsome in a subtle way. He had thinning blond hair and something of a weak mouth. He came up to them with a concerned look on his face. "Did something happen?" he asked.

Ramsay seemed to want to wait to answer the question. Instead, he asked, "Are you Harlowe Cooper?"

The man nodded. "I am."

Ramsay said, "I'm Ramsay Downey."

"The police chief?" Harlowe's face looked baffled. "What's going on here?"

"Have you been in the house for the last couple of hours?" asked Ramsay.

Harlowe nodded again, this time more impatiently. "I've been asleep. I just woke up at the sound of your car pulling in. Where's Summer?"

Ramsay said slowly, "I'm very sorry to have to tell you this, but your wife is dead."

Harlowe staggered back a step, his eyes huge. "What? No. Summer's fine—I saw her this morning when she got up. Have you been in the studio? Her opening day is today."

He took a couple of steps toward the studio before Ramsay stopped him. "I'm sorry, but the studio is off-limits right now."

Now Harlowe's voice sounded panicked. "How do you know it's Summer? It could be someone else. Maybe one of her clients had a heart attack or something. It could be someone else."

Ramsay shook his head and gently said, "Is there a place we can sit you down?"

Harlowe plopped himself down immediately at the suggestion, practically falling on the stone steps leading from the house down to the studio.

"Is there anyone I can call to be with you?" asked Ramsay.

Harlowe shook his head, his teeth chattering slightly.

"I've got blankets in my car," said Piper, looking glad for something to do.

Beatrice gingerly sat down next to Harlowe on the stone step and put a hand on his knee. "It'll be all right. It's just the shock."

Piper returned quickly with a pile of baby quilts and blankets, which she proceeded to put over Harlowe. She also found an unopened plastic water bottle, which she offered him. He accepted it gratefully, draining half of it in a few gulps.

"What happened?" asked Harlowe finally, in a dull voice.

"That's what I was hoping you could help me with," said Ramsay. "All I know right now is your wife was murdered with a blunt object. She was discovered by Piper and Beatrice, who arrived to take advantage of a group class."

Harlowe looked vaguely at Piper and Beatrice as if having a hard time making connections. "You were clients."

Piper said, "We were planning on trying out the class. We're so sorry, Harlowe."

Harlowe rubbed his eyes.

Ramsay said, "Did you see or hear anything this morning that might help give us an idea as to what happened?"

In a muted voice that Beatrice had to strain to hear, Harlowe said, "I didn't hear a thing. I registered when Summer got up for the day, but then I fell back asleep. I was pretty worn out with the storm last night keeping me up for a while. I think I heard a tree fall on the property, too, at some point. We have a white noise machine in our bedroom because I'm usually a light sleeper and sounds like dogs barking will keep me up for hours. I never fall back asleep." He added bitterly. "Except for this morning. Except for when Summer needed me."

"Can you tell me a little about Summer?" asked Ramsay. "Give me a little background on the two of you?"

Harlowe took a deep, shaky breath. In that same quiet voice, he said, "We met back in college. Summer was just so pretty and so impressive. She had a lot of drive . . . with everything. She made dean's list, was in a sorority, and even played club sports for the school."

"Did she? Which sports?" asked Piper.

Beatrice could tell Piper was encouraging Harlowe to speak about Summer, because it seemed to be helping him with the shock. She saw a smile hovering around Harlowe's lips as he remembered.

"The sports? Oh, there were lots of them. Everything from soccer to kickball. Plus, she'd gotten a scholarship to the school because of women's softball. I was never athletic, and I was shy about approaching Summer because I didn't feel like much of a catch. She always seemed to be in the middle of a group of friends, too. But she was just so amazing that I somehow managed to summon the courage to approach her when I spotted her on her own for a few minutes."

Beatrice thought he was selling himself short. Harlowe was handsome in a quiet way.

"I wasn't ever sure really what she saw in me." He shrugged a shoulder and looked blankly at the crime tape surrounding the studio, as if he couldn't quite figure out how he'd gotten from happy college memories to a crime scene.

Ramsay said, "How did the two you end up in Dappled Hills? Did your work bring you here?"

Harlowe looked at him, almost as if he'd forgotten he was there. "The house had been in my family—it was a vacation home for my grandmother. She lived in Florida most of the year, but would come to Dappled Hills in the summers to get some relief from the heat."

Ramsay nodded. "I think I remember meeting her a few times."

"She left it to me in her will when I was still in school. Summer and I thought it was the perfect place to move after we graduated from college and got married. It would mean we wouldn't have a mortgage payment. The house needed a little work, for sure. My grandmother hadn't neglected it, but she hadn't been here most of the year to take care of regular maintenance. Summer had money and was able to fix it up."

"Summer was wealthy, even back then?" Ramsay was eyeing the expensive new studio as if it was all coming together.

Harlowe nodded. "She had family money to start out with, but then she made her own on top of that." He added proudly, "She was a whiz at the stock market. I mean, she did have money to invest, which helps, but then she *grew* it. She had a real knack for investing and loved reading up on stocks and figuring out what the market might do. Anyway, she fixed up the house with some of her earnings and made it look amazing. It hadn't been much before she got her hands on it."

Ramsay said, "Thinking back on what happened this morning. Is there anyone you can come up with who might have had cause to harm Summer? Was there anybody she mentioned who she'd been arguing with? Any tension with someone?"

Harlowe was silent for a few moments to consider this. "There was some sort of conflict between Summer and the contractor who was helping us build the studio. What was his name? Oh, that's right—Dan."

Beatrice winced. Dan Whitner was dating fellow quilter Tiggy and was considered a friend of the group. He was a quiet man who'd done a lot of work for the church.

Ramsay took out a small notebook. "So Dan was helping you out with the construction. That seems like a major project."

Harlowe said, "He was, but he wasn't the only one. I was sort of overseeing the whole project for Summer." He gave a short laugh. "Well, I was *supposed* to be. Summer was something of a perfectionist and she had a hard time delegating tasks to other people. Often, she was down at the studio herself, taking stock of how it was going. Technically, though, that was my job."

Ramsay jotted that down. "I guess the grocery store was being flexible with your hours. You're the manager there, aren't you?"

Harlowe said, "Well, I was. I quit my job there just a couple of months ago." He sighed, rubbing his eyes. "I guess I'm going to have to ask to be rehired now. But I think they filled my old job."

Ramsay quirked an eyebrow. "You quit? Problems at the store?"

Harlowe shook his head. "Nothing like that. Summer had asked if I would work for her instead. I resigned and immediately started helping her out."

Beatrice frowned. Harlowe didn't quite seem to fit the mold of a fitness instructor. He was certainly thin enough, but he didn't look remotely athletic. And he'd admitted the same thing himself just minutes ago.

Harlowe elaborated, seeing their confused expressions. "Sorry. I mean, I was working for Summer in the *office*. I wasn't planning on teaching classes or anything. I was managing the books and that sort of thing. And, like I mentioned, overseeing the construction work. The next step was advertising, which I was just getting started on."

Ramsay said, "And you weren't happy with Dan's work."

"Well, it was more that Summer wasn't. But if Summer wasn't happy, nobody was happy." He teared up for a second and paused for a moment to get control of himself again. He finally said, "She was quite a businesswoman. Summer liked things to run on schedule."

"And the construction of the studio wasn't going according to plan?"

Harlowe shrugged. "Not up to Summer's standards, anyway. She wasn't happy with the rate of progress. Naturally, she wanted to have the studio ready to go so she could start her classes. She wasn't happy with the fact that Dan had other projects he was juggling at the same time. What's more, she didn't think he'd done a good job with the plumbing work."

"Was he fired from the job?" asked Ramsay.

Harlowe nodded unhappily. "Like I said, Summer was something of a perfectionist. She wasn't happy with Dan's pace or his work, so she decided she had to let him go. The only problem was that Dappled Hills isn't very big and there aren't a lot of general contractors here. We had a delay while we found somebody. Plus, we had to get on their calendar. Summer opened the studio as early as she could, but it was much later than she expected. And not everything is completed." He rubbed his face and muttered, "And now, it never will be."

"What are your plans now?" asked Ramsay, looking curiously at him. "Are you planning on continuing with the studio?"

Harlowe gave a short laugh. "How can I?"

Piper said, "You could always hire instructors to work here. Then you could still manage the business side of things."

Harlowe sighed. "That makes the most sense, of course. But it's so hard to imagine my life here in Dappled Hills without Summer. She was the whole reason I was here to begin with. She was the one who thought my grandmother's place could be made into a wonderful home. I'm going to have a lot of memories to sort through. Besides, I'm not even sure if I can find work. They found somebody for my job at the grocery, like I was saying."

There was the sound of cars pulling into the gravel parking lot above and Ramsay said, "That'll be the state police. Harlowe, if you could stick around in case they'd like to speak with you, I would appreciate it."

"Should we wait, too?" asked Piper.

Ramsay shook his head. "I think I've gotten enough of a statement from you two. You've probably got to get back to Will so Ash can go to work. If any more questions come up, I'll reach out to you."

And so, Beatrice and Piper headed back to their cars.

Chapter Four

"This was not exactly what I planned for this morning," said Piper, making a face. "I'm sorry to drag you into this, Mama."

"Oh, I'm glad to have been here with you. It would have been awful for you to face that on your own."

Piper gave a little shudder at the thought of going solo into the studio and finding Summer there in that silent place. "Poor Summer."

Beatrice looked at her curiously. "What did you think of her?"

Piper sighed. "Well, I hate speaking ill of the dead, but I honestly had a tough time warming up to Summer. I always felt sort of overwhelmed by her."

"She had a big personality?"

Piper nodded. "That, and the fact she was totally passionate about what she was doing. I mean, she lived, breathed, and ate fitness. She really walked the walk. Whenever I saw her at the store, she was buying superfoods. She kept trying to get me to come to one of her classes when she was working in Lenoir. But I never made it over there."

"Because of your schedule?"

"That was part of it. Mornings are a little tight at our house and driving all the way to Lenoir wasn't really going to fit in. But part of the reason might be because I liked Danica a lot better. If I *did* drive to Lenoir, I would want to go to Danica's classes, not Summer's. And I'm sure that would really have irritated Summer."

Beatrice frowned. "Danica. I'm not sure if I know her."

"She's great, actually. Always really approachable about health and fitness. With Summer, I kind of felt overwhelmed when she'd talk about it—it was like it was the end-all and be-all for her. Danica seems to have a more moderate approach to it. She'd talk about taking baby steps toward a healthier body."

"Is Danica teaching locally?" asked Beatrice.

Piper shook her head. "Actually, I haven't seen her around much at all lately. But the last I heard, she was teaching classes in Lenoir with Summer. Anyway, with Summer's studio the only real place to go here in Dappled Hills, I figured I'd try it out." She glanced at her watch. "Sorry, Mama, but I've got to head out. Ash needs to go to work and I've got to get Will to preschool so I can run over to the school."

Beatrice gave her daughter a hug and waved to her as she drove off. Then she climbed into her own car and headed back home.

Wyatt was startled when she walked inside the house. So was Noo-noo . . . she gave a surprised yip when Beatrice entered. Then the little corgi wiggled her rear to indicate that she was very pleased to see her.

"That was a quick workout," said Wyatt, still eating his bowl of cereal. He frowned. "You don't even look sweaty. Wasn't it a rigorous class at all?"

"We didn't end up having the class," said Beatrice, reaching down to pet Noo-noo. She drew in a deep breath. "The instructor was dead."

"What?" Wyatt rose from his chair and walked over to Beatrice, pulling out a chair for her. "Here, sit down."

Wyatt waited, not wanting to rush her. After a few moments, Beatrice said, "Piper and I walked into the studio and Summer was lying there on the floor. Someone had come in and beaten her with a hand weight."

She shivered, and Wyatt pulled his chair up close and put his arm around her. "I'm so sorry," he said softly.

Beatrice nodded. "It was the shock of it all. I mean, I didn't even know Summer, of course. She was just the person who was to teach the exercise class I was trying out."

Wyatt shook his head. "It doesn't matter if you knew her or not. It was still a pretty traumatizing experience. Do you want to talk about it? Or would you rather lie down for a little while? Maybe with Noo-noo?"

Noo-noo, who'd sensed Beatrice's heavy mood and had been lying with her head on Beatrice's foot, looked hopeful at the thought.

Beatrice considered this. "Maybe I'll talk about it and *then* go lie down. A little of both. It was an early start this morning to get ready for the class, and now I'm totally exhausted without even having exercised at all." She took a deep breath. "After Piper and I found Summer, we called Ramsay right away."

"Did he make it there quickly?"

Beatrice nodded. "Very. No one else was there—I guess Summer hadn't gotten the chance to do any advertising. It sounded like she was very involved in the day-to-day construction and getting the studio set up. Anyway, Piper and I walked in and found her. It had been silent in the studio—sort of eerie."

Wyatt shook his head sadly. "I'm so sorry."

"It's very sad. She was a young woman and, from everything I've heard, very excited about her new studio. Her husband came outside and spoke to us for a few minutes. Harlowe. He seemed very shaken by it. He managed the business end of things."

"That must have been a nasty shock for him, too." Wyatt looked at her with concern. "Here, why don't you put your feet up for a little while?" he said as he led her to the bedroom. "Noo-noo can have a nap, too."

Noo-noo's ears perked up and her sweet face looked at Beatrice with concern. She trotted after her as Beatrice took off her shoes and hopped into bed. The little dog hopped up onto the bed with her and quickly curled up next to Beatrice.

Wyatt came back into the room a few minutes later with a motley assortment of things to eat and drink. "I wasn't sure you had eaten anything this morning."

"I'd thought I'd wait until after I'd exercised. Then I totally forgot. I'm not feeling very hungry, though."

Wyatt carefully put a glass of ice water next to the bed and then handed her a plate with a piece of toast with strawberry jam and a scrambled egg to its side.

"Actually," admitted Beatrice, "that looks pretty good."

"Can I bring you anything else?" he asked, reaching out to gently push a stray tendril of her white-blonde hair to the side.

"No, I'm perfect."

He grinned at her. "I'd agree." He quietly left her with the corgi and she ate the breakfast with Noo-noo watching her with interest.

She picked up her book after she finished eating. It might not be the very best book to be reading, under the circumstances. Ramsay and she had a sort of unofficial book club where they recommended books to each other and then would spend some time talking about why they liked them. He'd recommended an Agatha Christie book she hadn't read yet: *By the Pricking of my Thumbs*. Beatrice remembered she hadn't for some reason been a huge Tommy and Tuppence fan, but she found this book engrossing so far. It was also very scary. Scary enough that she didn't take the little nap that she'd thought she would.

Wyatt stuck his head into the room to check on her. "Not sleepy?"

Beatrice shook her head. "It's this book. It has a very ominous and unsettling tone to it. I guess I should be reading something a bit lighter. Maybe a beach book. I think I'm going to get up and make my way over to the Patchwork Cottage since I have a couple of things I want to pick up there. Are you heading out to the church?"

Wyatt nodded. "I have a meeting in about twenty minutes. Call me if you need anything or want to hang out with me at the church."

Beatrice gave him a grin. "I'm not sure some of the folks would appreciate that very much. The minister's wife just lounging around the church. They'd probably find something productive for me to do. Or I'd end up on some committee."

Wyatt chuckled. "Maybe. But do call me if you need me."

He left for his meeting and Beatrice put on some makeup, let Noo-noo out, and then headed off in her car for downtown

Dappled Hills. It was a beautiful day, which made the events of the morning seem particularly unreal. People were out on bikes or walking their dogs down the tree-lined streets. A banner was strung over the street to advertise the upcoming craft and music festival. It looked like a chamber of commerce day in Dappled Hills.

Walking into the Patchwork Cottage always gave Beatrice a bit of a lift. Not only was it where her good friend Posy worked, but it was a cheerful, relaxing environment. Posy always had fresh baked goods out for customers, there was a plump and friendly store cat named Maisie, and music from local musicians played softly in the background.

Posy smiled at her. "Good morning!"

"Too late for that, I think," said Beatrice wryly.

Posy's eyes opened wide. "You know about Summer Cooper, then?"

"I can tell the news is already making the rounds. Piper and I were actually the ones who found her."

Posy's kind blue eyes clouded over. "Oh no. How awful. I didn't really know her, but when I saw her out in town, she looked like such a vibrant woman."

"I think she was. And very young, too." Beatrice shook her head. "And here I am dwelling on it again. I actually came over to try to distract myself."

Posy, sensing a mission, hopped on it. "I can help with that. How are things going with your projects?"

"Not so bad. I do need to finish up, though. I've had a lot of quiet time lately and have been doing plenty of quilting and reading. The only problem is, I tend to cross quilting off my list when I'm not *technically* done. If I don't get back on it, I'll be doing a last-minute desperate session to get it finished before the guild meeting."

The bell to the store rung and fellow quilter and Beatrice's co-grandmother Meadow burst through the door. Beatrice sighed. She and Meadow were good friends, but Meadow was something of a force of nature sometimes. Beatrice wasn't altogether sure she could handle a full Meadow experience that morning.

As soon as Meadow spotted her, she rushed over. "I *hoped* you were going to be here. Mercy!"

"Piper must have spoken with you," guessed Beatrice.

"She certainly did. You know Ramsay didn't. How *awful*. I'm surprised you didn't take to your bed this morning. Did you hear about Summer, Posy?"

Posy nodded sadly. "Actually, Beatrice was just saying she was looking for a distraction from it all."

"Well, of *course* you are! How absolutely terrible." Meadow frowned ferociously, as if trying to think of a distraction suitable enough to counter a murder. Then she beamed. "Quilting! How is your UFO swap going, Beatrice?"

She chuckled. "I'm not so sure. Poor Piper has my unfinished project and I don't understand how she has time to sleep, much less quilt. I may have to take it back from her. And I've got her unfinished quilt, which is almost done. How about you?"

Posy chuckled. "Wait until you hear who she swapped with."

Meadow looked smug. "Savannah ended up with one of my unfinished objects. It's a crazy quilt."

Beatrice bet it was. When Meadow was trying to use up old fabric, anything went. But Meadow was such an adept quilter that she could make the wildest combination work. She frowned. "Does Savannah even *have* any UFOs? She seems totally compulsive about finishing her projects."

Meadow laughed. "Knowing her, I strongly suspect she had to start something in order for me to finish it. It's probably driving her crazy, too. I don't think this is her favorite guild activity."

Posy said, "Probably not. I'm not sure June Bug had anything unfinished, either."

Beatrice shook her head. "She's a workhorse. June Bug absolutely amazes me. She plows through baking, business, quilting. I can't even picture her relaxing or at rest."

"I think she likes it that way, though," said Posy thoughtfully. "She never seems unhappy or dissatisfied."

This was true. June Bug always had a pleased expression on her face, as if her world was one full of happy things.

Meadow said, "I'm going to have to be a workhorse myself if I'm going to get Savannah's quilt done in time for the meeting. Can you imagine how agitated she'd be if hers wasn't completed?"

"I think she'd reclaim it," said Beatrice with a smile.

"Maybe I can quilt some when Will is over playing," said Meadow thoughtfully.

Beatrice found this highly unlikely. Meadow used every bit of time she had with Will to interact with him. His visits with her were full of reading, playing, and eating snacks together. Unless Will was napping, she couldn't imagine Meadow quilting.

The bell on the door rang and a thin older woman walked in, bearing a cane. Posy quickly walked her way. "Sylvia! It's so good to see you. What can I help you with today?"

But Sylvia's gaze was fixed on Beatrice. "You were there to-day?"

"Where?" asked Beatrice with a frown.

"At my neighbor's house. With the dead woman."

Posy turned and gave Beatrice an apologetic look. It was apparently going to be tougher to be distracted today than she'd thought.

"You live next to Summer and Harlowe?"

Sylvia looked impatiently at Beatrice. "Yes. It's been horrid lately, with all the construction going on. People working over there all hours of the day and night. Noise all the time. My poor Cammie has been at her wit's end."

"Cammie?" asked Beatrice with a frown.

The old woman reached into her large purse and pulled out a small dog who blinked sleepily and gave Beatrice a disdainful look, as if blaming her for the interruption of her naptime.

Posy said sympathetically, "All the construction must have been very upsetting to Cammie."

Sylvia nodded. "She's been barking and whining for weeks. I was so very relieved when most of the work appeared to be over. But then, this morning, I saw all the emergency vehicles and walked over."

Meadow said, "You must have spoken with my husband. Ramsay."

Sylvia pursed her lips. "I'm not sure who it was I spoke with. Whoever it was told me an abbreviated version of what had happened. I was hoping you could fill me in, since you'd been there."

Her gaze pierced Beatrice. "I probably don't know much more than you do, to be honest."

Sylvia said in a clipped voice, "You know who's dead."

"Yes. Unfortunately, it's your neighbor—Summer."

Sylvia gave a bob of her head as if this news didn't come as any sort of surprise at all.

"We were actually trying to distract Beatrice from thinking about it," said Meadow with one of her jolliest smiles. "Maybe you can help us do that."

Now Sylvia looked just as disdainful as her Cammie had moments before. "You have to learn to control your emotions."

"Yes, I should work on that," said Beatrice dryly. She paused. "I don't suppose you saw anything happen next door this morning?"

"I saw quite a lot happen next door. So much that I started to ignore it." Sylvia pursed her lips. "Those two didn't get along very well."

"Harlowe and Summer, you mean?"

"Whatever their names are," said Sylvia with a sniff. "Always arguing. Loudly. I wondered if they simply assumed I must be deaf at my age. They'd fuss with each other all the time."

Posy's eyes were huge. "Harlowe didn't seem violent toward Summer, did he? Do you think he was the one who killed her?"

"I think Summer was far more likely to kill Harlowe. She was the one who was on his case all the time. Her entire manner was very patronizing toward him. As if she were in control and he was some sort of minion. A very unsatisfactory minion."

Meadow had been gaping at Sylvia as she unveiled the Baxters' private life. "Did you see anything this morning, though? Maybe Harlowe got fed up with being treated that way and sneaked down and murdered her?"

Sylvia said, "If there's something I know about this morning, I'll keep it to myself. I'm not one to engage in any tittle-tattle."

Beatrice thought entirely the opposite. Sylvia had been dishing on Summer and Harlowe's marriage just moments before.

"And now, if you'll excuse me, Cammie and I need to get my fabric and then head back home. She'll need her walk and her morning nap." With that, Sylvia swept away with Posy scuttling behind her to give her a hand.

Chapter Five

Meadow watched them leave with her eyebrows high. "I do believe Sylvia knows something."

Beatrice shrugged. "Maybe she's the sort of person who likes to know things. I only hope she tells Ramsay about it."

Meadow said, "I'll ask Ramsay to go talk with her again. Maybe she'll give the police more information than she gave us." Then she added, "And now we're not going to talk about this anymore! We're supposed to be distracting you."

A large snore came from the corner of the store.

Meadow chuckled, "Miss Sissy was getting grouchy about people disturbing her naps in the sitting area, so Posy set up an armchair with an ottoman in the back corner. Miss Sissy has been curled up there ever since."

Miss Sissy was an elderly and rather irascible quilter who often spent time at Posy's shop.

"And Maisie, too?" Beatrice hadn't spotted the shop cat yet.

"Don't you know it? She's back there in the corner with Miss Sissy. They're peas in a pod. Now, let's talk about my most-favorite subject."

"Cooking?" asked Beatrice with a grin. She knew exactly what Meadow's favorite subject was, but decided to tease her co-grandmother.

"Cooking? Heavens no. I can't imagine what you're thinking, Beatrice. *Will* is my favorite subject. You'll love seeing my latest video of him," pronounced Meadow, whipping her phone out of her purse.

Meadow had taught Will to sing the alphabet song. He did do a marvelous job, decided Beatrice, despite the fact he had a bit of trouble around *k*. He'd also created an entirely new letter, *lmnop* which ran together quite charmingly as he sang the song.

"He'll be the star in his preschool class," said Meadow smugly. "He's clearly very, very bright."

Beatrice, naturally, agreed. She was a grandmother, after all.

"What are your plans for the rest of the day?" asked Meadow.

Beatrice considered this. "Well, after I pick up my supplies here, I'd better get to work on finishing Piper's UFO. Then I think I'll try to take a nap—my efforts were unsuccessful last time, but maybe quilting will relax me a bit."

"Good idea," said Meadow, who always thought quilting was a good idea.

"And, of course, it's Monday," said Beatrice.

Meadow's eyes opened wide. "Is it? Goodness, but it sneaked up on me. So you'll have church tonight then. Youth group, Bible studies, and whatnot."

The church had Wednesday night activities but was currently running a special Monday night program, with Bible studies focusing on a particular theme.

Beatrice nodded. "And I should be able to handle it all, after a good nap this afternoon."

And that's how Beatrice's day progressed. She bought her materials at the shop, headed back home, quilted until she got drowsy, took a nap with Noo-noo snuggled up against her and gently snoring, woke up, tried to make sense of her hair after the nap, and then headed over to the church.

Beatrice was actually getting a lot from the Monday night program they were running. There were tons of young people there, all engaged in conversation and activities. Often, she'd lend a hand in the kitchen with either food prep or clean-up, or stand in the serving line and dish out the dinner offerings. Wyatt led a Bible study class, and she'd sit in to listen to him.

This time, she decided to help out with clean-up after the spaghetti supper. It was a fairly easy task and the clean-up crew was always chatty. Tobi Daxton was the other woman in the kitchen with Beatrice, loading the commercial dishwasher as Beatrice scraped plates. Tobi was a Sunday school teacher at the church for the elementary program and was involved in various other activities, too. Her husband, Quinn, was also very involved at the church and on several committees.

Tobi said, "You do the Pilates class here, don't you, Beatrice?"

Beatrice nodded as she handed her a pan to put in the dishwasher. "I do, to the best of my ability, anyway. Sometimes my legs don't seem to want to make the circles that the instructor wants them to. But I feel like the class helps make me stronger, so I'm trying to keep up with it. It's only once a week. I don't think I can handle anything more vigorous than that."

Tobi said, "That sounds good. I need to start out slow and easy. I was going to go into total bootcamp mode and do one of Summer Cooper's programs, but it didn't work out."

From Tobi's expression, Beatrice could tell Tobi knew Beatrice had been at the scene that morning. She sighed. "It sure didn't work out, did it? Poor Summer."

"What exactly happened?" asked Tobi. She flushed a little and quickly said, "I hope you don't think I want to gossip about it, but the truth is that Summer and I were friendly with each other."

"Oh, I'm sorry," said Beatrice. "Her death must have come as a real shock."

"It did. I mean, Summer and I weren't best friends or any-thing, but we socialized a little in town . . . it's hard not to in a town this size. I was actually trying to persuade Summer to visit the church."

Beatrice thought Tobi sounded very matter-of-fact about Summer's sudden death. She adopted the same tone and said, "Well, there's not very much to tell. Piper and I were planning on taking one of Summer's free trial group classes this morning. We'd gotten there fairly early and walked into the studio."

"Was the studio nice?" asked Tobi in a rather wistful voice. "I heard she was putting a lot of work into it."

Beatrice nodded. "It seemed really nice, although I didn't register too much about the building itself."

"Of course not," said Tobi quickly. She paused. "I heard it was really early in the morning."

"It was to be the first class of the day. And, I suppose, the first class for the studio."

Tobi sighed. "I didn't hear about Summer's death for a while this morning. I was sleeping in, then I didn't really check my phone or run any errands, so it took forever for me to find out about it. Pretty amazing when you think about how fast gossip travels in Dappled Hills."

"It must have been a shock to hear the news, especially since you and Summer were friends. Such a terrible thing—here she was about to realize her dream and her life was ripped from her. Hopefully, the police will be able to have some good leads as to who is responsible."

Tobi nodded. "I've been thinking about it, too, just trying to think who might have done something like that. At first, I thought it must have been some random person breaking in, looking for money or something."

"That's pretty unlikely, I think. After all, the studio was all lit up and visible from the outside because it was so early in the morning. A thief would have been able to see it was all workout equipment in there."

Tobi said, "That's when I started looking at whether it might be someone Summer knew. I'm sure poor Harlowe is probably suspect number one with the police. On TV, the husband is always the prime suspect, anyway."

"I think that's probably the case in real life, too."

"But anybody who knows Harlowe would find that hard to believe. Did you meet him?" asked Tobi.

Beatrice nodded and Tobi continued, "He doesn't fit the part of the murdering husband. Plus, I always got the impression that Summer sort of intimidated Harlowe. I think any money they had was Summer's money. Harlowe worked at the grocery store before quitting to work for Summer. Somehow, I just can't see him doing something like this."

Beatrice handed Tobi another pan to put in the commercial dishwasher. "Is there someone else you think could have harmed Summer?"

Tobi glanced around to make sure it was still only the two of them in the space. "I don't know the whole story, but Remi Kingston and Summer had a big fight with each other not too long ago. I'm not sure why it happened. They used to be really good friends and then they suddenly stopped talking to each other. There's got to be a story behind that."

Then Tobi gave her an apologetic smile. "Sorry. We should probably be talking about nicer topics than this at the church. How's that adorable dog of yours?"

"Noo-noo? She's as sweet as ever. She always seems to know what I'm feeling. Earlier today, she curled up right next to me to cheer me up."

Tobi said, "Aww! Dogs give the best snuggles ever."

There was plenty of dog fur on Tobi's outfit to attest to this statement. They chatted happily about everything dog-related for a while, with Tobi talking about a particular trail she walked her dog on that she thought might be fun for Beatrice and Noo-noo. Then Tobi said, "While you're here, Beatrice, there was one thing I wanted to ask you about. I had some ideas for the youth program—the younger kids. I'm a little hesitant about passing them on since I'm not even a parent yet, although I want to be one."

Beatrice said, "Oh, Wyatt loves hearing about new ideas. He's always looking for ways to improve the youth programming."

Tobi smiled. "That's great to hear. I really think it could be fun for the youth and it looks like other churches are doing something similar."

"I'll ask Wyatt to reach out to you. He'll want to schedule a meeting with you and someone from the youth committee."

They chatted for a bit longer before finishing the meal clean-up. Tobi headed off to speak with someone else, and Beatrice straightened chairs in the church hall.

Her friend Mellie, a fellow quilter, came up to join her. Beatrice smiled at her. "Hey there. I was thinking about you the other day and wondering how your online quilt shop is working out."

Mellie looked pleased. "Well, with Posy's help, it's doing pretty well! I have as much work as I can keep up with. And I get a lot of satisfaction in helping to put together someone's idea."

"I'm guessing some of them give you more instructions than others?"

Mellie nodded. "Sometimes they'll just say they need a baby quilt for an expectant mother. But sometimes, they'll say they want it to be a particular shade of blue and have a certain type of duck on it or the baby's name."

"Those folks must be harder to handle. It would be tough to deliver exactly what they'd envisioned."

Mellie said, "So far I haven't had anyone complain about a completed quilt. Fingers crossed it stays that way." She paused. "I wanted to tell you that I was sorry about you and Piper finding Summer this morning. Walking into that scene must have upset y'all so much. Are you both okay?"

"Much better than poor Summer," said Beatrice with a grimace. "Piper and I are fine. It was just startling. Did you know Summer well?"

Mellie shook her head. "Not really. We moved in different circles, I guess. I *need* to exercise. I'm sure my stress level would probably go down if I did. But the kind of classes Summer held weren't really beginner-friendly, I don't think. From what I saw on her website, anyway."

Beatrice said wryly, "I had the feeling that might be the case. Piper had persuaded me to go to a trial class with her. But the exercise classes here at the church are probably more my speed."

"I keep forgetting about those. I need to set an alarm for myself. By the time I remember the class, it's already halfway finished." She paused. "I saw you and Tobi were talking with each other in the kitchen."

Beatrice nodded. "Just catching up with each other. Tobi has some ideas for the youth program here." She wasn't about to disclose that they'd been talking about Summer's sudden demise.

Mellie swallowed. "I've been trying to decide what to do. You know the last thing I want is to be involved in another murder case."

Mellie's family had been the focus of an investigation not long ago. Beatrice said, "Oh, I have no doubt." Mellie looked so concerned and nervous that Beatrice said, "How about if we take a seat for a few minutes?"

Mellie accepted that idea with relief and they headed to a remote area of the hall where no one was around.

Mellie said, "It's probably nothing, anyway. But I was wondering if I needed to tell Ramsay about it just in case. What do you think I should do?"

"Why not tell me about it? Maybe it'll make you feel better to share it with somebody. Did you talk with your husband about it?"

Mellie shook her head. "He got a new job after so many months of looking for one. It's hard to find management work around here. He's just finished up with the training program and all the human resources stuff. I can't dump something like this on him."

"That's sweet of you to try to spare him any worries."

Mellie gave her a small smile. "Anyway, I was out having a conversation with Tobi outside the Patchwork Cottage not long before Summer died. Everything was fine and we were passing the time. Summer walked by and gave Tobi this really smug look."

"A smug look?"

"Yes. And Tobi practically snarled at her in response. I had no idea what was going on because one second, we were making pleasantries and then suddenly there was all this subtext that I didn't understand."

Beatrice said, "Did you ask Tobi about it?"

Mellie nodded. "I felt nosy, but I was so startled that I asked. Then I felt even *worse* because Tobi started crying. Then I quickly told her it was none of my business and changed the subject."

"And when exactly was that?'

Mellie sighed, "It was a couple of days ago. Do you think I need to let Ramsay know? It might not even be anything. Besides, I don't even completely understand what I was witnessing except that there were bad feelings between Summer and Tobi."

Beatrice said, "Based on what you've told me, I think it might be a good idea to let Ramsay know. He can decide if the information is important or not."

"Like I said, I'm sure Tobi would never do anything to Summer. But I've still had this on my mind. Thanks for your advice, Beatrice."

Beatrice smiled at her. "You're doing the right thing. Ramsay is always fair, and he wouldn't be able to act on the information unless there's evidence against Tobi."

Mellie changed the subject to happier things, and they chatted for a while about their quilting projects. Beatrice was wryly saying she needed to get some quilting in so she could finish Piper's UFO or else she'd have to pay Mellie to do it since Mellie had gone pro. She'd had every intention of finishing the quilt that afternoon, but nap had attacked her and pulled her away from it.

They were laughing when Mellie leaned forward and said in a low voice, "Don't look now, but somebody's really giving you a dirty look."

Naturally, Beatrice couldn't resist turning around. Sure enough, Miss Sissy was giving her a glare that could have curdled milk. Beatrice smiled at her and turned back around again.

"What did you do to Miss Sissy?" breathed Mellie.

Beatrice chuckled. "I'm guessing she's mad because I don't have my grandson with me. Miss Sissy considers me practically worthless unless I have Will in tow."

"Does Miss Sissy have a UFO assigned to her for the guild meeting?"

Beatrice said, "Now that is a good question. Often Miss Sissy flies under the radar at the meetings whenever we're doing various swaps. When it comes time to get an assignment, she'll give this steely look that prevents anyone from giving her anything. Maybe I can get her to finish Piper's project if I can get the last little bit done."

"Is she a good quilter?" asked Mellie, looking doubtful.

"Oh yes. She's a master quilter. Her house is a treasure trove of projects."

She and Mellie chatted for a few more minutes before she joined up with Wyatt again. Soon it was time to leave and try to unwind after a long, and rather odd day.

Chapter Six

Despite trying every trick in the book, Beatrice couldn't fall asleep that night. Images from the morning kept popping up, unbidden, in her mind. She stumbled out of the bedroom, reassuring a sleepy Wyatt who asked if she was okay, and curled up on the sofa with Noo-noo and her book.

Unfortunately, *By the Pricking of my Thumbs* was probably not the book to be reading if you wanted to erase a murder from your head. She was riveted to the story and kept turning pages until she reached the shocking conclusion. Then she glanced up at the wall clock and was startled to find that it was three o'clock in the morning. Noo-noo gave Beatrice a worried look, as if she knew it was far past Beatrice's bedtime.

"Okay, I'm going to go to sleep for real this time," proclaimed Beatrice to the little dog. Noo-noo seemed doubtful.

Falling asleep proved to be slow-going, but she finally managed to catch a few winks as the sun was just starting to shine through the windows. Fortunately, Wyatt, mindful of her restless night, thoughtfully slipped out of the bed, got ready for work, and left without waking her up.

When Beatrice finally blearily checked the time, she winced. It was ten in the morning. She stumbled out of bed to find a note from Wyatt in the kitchen saying he hoped she felt better and that Noo-noo had been fed and walked.

"He's the best," she said to Noo-noo, who appeared to agree.

Beatrice poured a cup of coffee from the pot Wyatt had made for her and then ate some leftover Quiche Lorraine from the day before. She decided she needed to try to wind down a little and pick out a more soothing book from the library. She also recalled that Remi, who Tobi had said argued with Summer, worked at the library. It could make for an interesting morning.

After doing some stretches and getting ready for the day, Beatrice set out for the library. It was a relaxing place in itself with a fireplace near the periodicals, lots of windows providing cheery light, and houseplants scattered around.

Remi, fortunately, was working that morning. She had red hair and beautiful porcelain skin that Beatrice envied. She smiled as Beatrice walked up to her.

"Good morning," she said. "Looking for a book, maybe? I know you always have one you're working on."

Beatrice nodded. "I stayed up all night reading an Agatha Christie and now I need a really peaceful read to calm myself down again."

Remi tilted her head to one side. "Is everything okay?"

It seemed like an excellent segue to asking Remi some questions. "Actually, I had a really tough day yesterday. My daughter and I found Summer Baxter at her studio."

Remi's pale skin seemed a shade lighter than it had before. "Oh, no. I heard about Summer, of course, but I didn't realize you were the one who discovered her. How awful that must have been."

"Not as awful as it was for Summer, but pretty disturbing. That's why I had such a tough time sleeping last night and pulled my book out. But the book wasn't the right choice, under the circumstances." She paused and said, "I understand you and Summer were friends—I'm sorry for your loss."

"Thanks. I was saddened when I heard the news. Summer and I used to be close friends once, but we grew apart over time. I opened the library yesterday morning. We don't open until nine, of course, but I'd gotten here early because I wanted to catch up on shelving books before we opened. I was shocked when one of our patrons filled me in later. Summer was so full of vitality that it's tough for me to wrap my head around the fact that she's gone. I hadn't seen much of her, lately. She was very invested in getting her studio set up, of course, and that was consuming most of her time and energy. Plus, I've been working so many hours here at the library that I haven't had a chance to get out much."

"Piper said much the same thing—that Summer was such a strong person."

Remi said, "I guess she was taken by surprise? I hope she didn't suffer at all."

Beatrice said, "This is going to sound harsh, but I understand she could be a pretty hard person to be around sometimes. I have to wonder if she made the wrong person angry."

Beatrice was worried Remi might ascribe to the "don't speak ill of the dead" principle. She was glad when Remi immediately nodded to acknowledge Beatrice's take on Summer.

"She could be hard. In fact, I had something of a run-in with Summer once. It's so petty that I feel kind of guilty over it now—I should have ignored the issue and continued being close to Summer. But you know how it is. Once you feel as if you've been betrayed, it's tough to trust the person again."

"Absolutely," said Beatrice. "I'm so sorry you were betrayed by a friend. That must have been so hurtful."

"Well, like I mentioned, it's pretty petty. You know Quinn and Tobi, don't you?"

Beatrice nodded. "I know them from church. Tobi is involved in lots of different activities there. Quinn is too, but I don't know him quite as well."

"I used to have a crush on Quinn before he and Tobi got involved. It's pretty obvious why," added Remi dryly. "He looks like a movie star. But I wasn't even that shallow—he's also a really avid reader."

"So he was in the library a lot, I'm guessing. What does he read?"

Remi shrugged. "Everything—nonfiction, mystery, literary fiction. Even poetry collections. Can you imagine reading poetry?"

Ramsay Downey immediately came to mind. Not only did the Dappled Hills police chief read poetry, he wrote it, too.

Beatrice said, "I like reading poetry, but mostly when I'm in a really reflective mood. Otherwise, I'm all about reading novels, as you know. Did Quinn have a favorite genre?"

"Southern gothic seemed to be the genre he liked the best. Anytime there was a new book in that genre, I let him know about it and sometimes we'd discuss the books. I wanted to date Quinn, but I felt very hesitant about it. Why would he want to go out with me?"

Beatrice said, "Why wouldn't he? You're smart and lovely."

Remi gave her a small smile. "That's generous of you. Anyway, Summer said she'd talk to Quinn and feel him out—see if he might be interested in going out to dinner with me. She said she knew him because they'd been neighbors at one point and had always been friendly. Summer came back to me later and said he must not have been 'the one' because he said he thought of me just as a friend and book guru."

"That must have stung," said Beatrice sympathetically.

"It did. But I totally got it. Like I said, I couldn't really think why he'd be interested in going out with me when he could date anybody he wanted to. I took Summer at her word that she'd talked with him about me."

"But she hadn't?" Beatrice raised her eyebrows.

"I never confirmed it with her, but I know she hadn't. For one thing, Quinn never behaved any differently with me when he came into the library. He was as warm as ever and didn't seem awkward at all. It was really confusing until I figured out that Summer must not have talked to him. Then he ended up dating Tobi and having a rushed engagement with her. I never really trusted Summer after that."

"But why would she have done that?"

Remi sighed. "I hate to say it, but Summer sometimes could be mean. I don't know if she even realized she was being mean. I think, in her mind, it was something of a game."

"That sounds even worse," said Beatrice.

"I know. The thing was, Summer wasn't stupid. In fact, she was probably one of the smartest people I know. But with that intelligence came a tendency toward boredom."

Beatrice said, "You think she messed with people's lives because she was bored?"

Beatrice must have sounded scandalized, because Remi gave her a reassuring smile. "Some people are just like that, you know? Anyway, I came to realize Quinn and I weren't meant to be. Since he and Tobi became engaged so quickly, they were clearly the ones who were supposed to be together. They obviously quickly fell in love. Even if Summer *had* talked to Quinn about me and he and I had started dating, it probably wouldn't have worked out. I guess I was spared some wasted time."

Beatrice thought Remi still looked wistful, though.

"Since you knew Summer, do you have any idea who might have done this?" asked Beatrice. "You said she could be mean. Was there anyone else she upset? Did she have any enemies?"

Remi considered this. "The one person who comes to mind is Danica." She held up a hand. "And I'm not saying Danica had anything to do with this. I really like her, actually."

"I haven't met Danica," Beatrice said. She remembered Piper talking about her, though, and how she'd have preferred taking fitness classes from Danica than from Summer.

"Danica Easton? She used to work with Summer. Summer was apparently responsible for Danica losing her job at the fitness center in Lenoir."

Beatrice raised her eyebrows. "Summer got her fired?"

"From what Danica told me. The only reason I know is because I was helping Danica look for a job with the library's job-hunting resources and Danica told me what happened. Danica was fired right before Summer quit to go work on building her own studio and Danica has been waitressing in Lenoir ever since then. Danica was very bitter about it, as you can imagine. Waitressing is just something she's doing in the meantime—she hasn't been able to find another job teaching fitness classes."

"Did you find out what happened?"

Remi said, "I don't really know the whole story. But Danica basically told me that Summer was responsible for her losing her job as a trainer. It sounded like Danica has been having a tough time." She gave a short laugh. "I shouldn't talk, though. I've been making use of the church's clothes closet and some other services."

Beatrice said, "That's what it's there for. Of course you should make use of it."

Remi gave her a smile. "Thanks. I'm just glad there's help available. I love this job, but sometimes what I make can't cover my expenses. Back to Danica, though—I hope she finds a job soon. She was talking about how much she missed teaching fitness classes."

"What a mess," said Beatrice, shaking her head.

"And totally unnecessary. Like I said, Summer seemed to do this kind of thing out of boredom. Anyway! I'm sorry I've been prattling on like this. You wanted to get a book recommendation, didn't you?"

Beatrice nodded. "Something a little lighter than what I'd been reading. Any ideas?"

Remi thought about it for a minute. "Have you read much Clyde Edgerton?"

"I've read *Walking Across Egypt*, and loved it."

Remi said, "Let's get you *Raney*. If you like his books, you should love that one."

Remi walked with her into the stacks and retrieved the book. Beatrice was going to try to chat with her more after she'd checked out the book, but just then a children's storytime let out and mothers and their kids were clamoring at the desk, wanting to check out their picture books. Beatrice left for home.

Chapter Seven

Not much later, she was out in the front yard weeding around her mailbox and trying to make sure she was staying out of the road in the process. She glanced up at the sound of a car and right as she did, Meadow startled her by honking her horn. Beatrice sighed as Meadow pulled up.

"Look at you, being all productive," said Meadow, grinning at her out the open window. Boris the dog was with her and he grinned too, drool dripping out the sides of his massive mouth.

"I'm trying," said Beatrice dryly. "If I don't keep on top of the weeds, they'll get out of control and then it's a lot more work to tackle them."

"Oh, I know, I know. If you still have some energy left, you should come by my house afterwards and pull some of *my* weeds."

Beatrice said, "I have the feeling I'm going to be ready to put my feet up after this, sad as that is. I suppose Ramsay isn't going to be much help in your yard now, what with the investigation."

"You have that right. Although I can't say he was a lot of help even before it! He seems to be under the delusion that Ash is going to come by and help us out in the yard. Ash! With a wife and baby! And a demanding job!"

Beatrice smiled at her. "He's a little busy right now, for sure. But then, so is Ramsay."

"I know. I've taken a few stabs at the yard myself, but like you're saying, if you neglect it even a tiny little bit, it's going to be an overwhelming job." She made a face. "Right now, I guess it's just Boris and me for company since Ramsay has barely even been home since this case started. There's got to be more of a balance between him being at home all the time and him *never* being home."

"Is Ramsay still thinking about retiring?" asked Beatrice. Although she thought Ramsay would absolutely love to retire, she couldn't help wonder who would step into his shoes. His deputy seemed competent, but not exactly a leader. And it was hard to think of an outsider to Dappled Hills being accepted by the community. Ramsay had been policing for a very long time and knew just about everybody by their first name.

Meadow nodded. "I think he needs some hobbies."

"But Ramsay *has* hobbies. He reads and writes. He *loves* reading and writing."

Meadow frowned. "The problem with those hobbies is that they're not the sort to get you out of the house. Ramsay needs some great out-of-the-house hobbies."

"Such as?"

"Golfing? I keep hearing about golf widows, and it sounds intriguing," said Meadow.

"I can't quite picture Ramsay out on the golf course. He'd be sitting in the cart and reading while his partners played."

Meadow sighed. "I suppose you're right. There's always the Rotary club, of course. Or he could get more involved with church."

"He's basically been working a service job for decades, though, and Ramsay always seems to recharge when he's holed up with a book," pointed out Beatrice.

Meadow made a face. "You're right about that. Sorry to complain. You know I think Ramsay is perfectly wonderful in every way. Except when he's underfoot. He also seems to have a cloud of clutter around him—notebooks, pens, half-read books, and snacks. Anyway, I guess I've just been cranky lately."

"Believe me, I understand. You should hear me ranting about the Cell Phone Guy at church."

Meadow rolled her eyes. "Don't get me started. Wyatt will be saying something so meaningful and lovely in the pulpit and then suddenly, out of nowhere, Ace Lincoln's phone starts buzzing. It totally wrecks the moment."

Meadow apparently decided it was time for a visit because she abruptly pulled into Beatrice's driveway and turned off her car's ignition. Beatrice removed her gardening gloves and said, "Let's head into the backyard, where we'll be more comfortable." She paused. "Is Boris doing better?" She had no desire for Boris to throw up the remainder of whatever he ate on the way through her house.

"He's *so* much better, thanks for asking. I told him he was a big boy for handling his tummy problems so stoically. But he's so ecstatic to be here that we'll just go through the gate instead of cutting through your house."

Boris was wildly excited. It was very fortunate that Meadow had him on a leash. Although, even leashed, he was prancing around in various directions, trying to figure out where he wanted to go first while Noo-noo watched with enormous eyes from inside the house.

Meadow disappeared with Boris through the gate into Beatrice's backyard while Beatrice retrieved Noo-noo from the house and let her into the backyard. She decided to bring some treats with her in case Boris needed a bit of bribing to be good.

Beatrice said as she walked outside, "Can I get you something to eat or drink?"

Meadow shook her head. "No thanks. What I'm more interested in is hearing about what you know about the case so far."

Boris bounced around like Tigger as Noo-noo watched, as if wondering what he was going to do next.

"Ramsay isn't giving you any information?"

Meadow snorted. "You know better than to ask that. As I mentioned, he's barely even home long enough for me to *be* nosy. But even if he was, he wouldn't tell me anything. He seems to think I'm indiscreet."

Meadow was the very definition of indiscretion, of course.

Beatrice said, "Well, I've spoken with a few people. Harlowe, of course, since he was right there when it happened. I've spoken with Tobi Daxton and Remi, too."

"I guess Ramsay's got to be ultra-focused on Harlowe, since he was Summer's husband. The spouse is always supposed to be the prime suspect."

Beatrice said, "I'm sure he is. But I will say Harlowe seemed genuinely shocked and upset when he learned about Summer's death. From all appearances, he was very supportive of her."

"I'll say. It's not every husband who leaves his job to work for his wife. He must have really believed in her studio. And in Summer, too."

Beatrice nodded. "And now he's having to look for another job."

"He's not interested in continuing to run the business himself?"

Beatrice said, "It would be tough to do without Summer. She was sort of the headliner for the whole thing. I guess he *could* find other instructors to work there and then oversee the business. But I don't think he'd make as much money doing that because he'd be channeling income to staff instead of to Summer."

Meadow considered this. "In that case, it seems pretty short-sighted for him to murder his main source of income."

"Right. I suppose it could have happened in the heat of the moment, but it still seems like a bad decision."

Meadow nodded. "And then you spoke with Tobi? I'm guessing at the church. I didn't make it there last night because I was still keeping an eye on Boris."

Boris grinned his doggy grin at her as if to say he knew she actually loved keeping an eye on him.

"He seems to be doing great," said Beatrice. "I'd never have guessed that he'd been into so much trouble."

Boris now grinned at Beatrice. She threw him a treat and then gave Noo-noo one.

Meadow said, "Is Tobi one of Ramsay's suspects?"

"Not as far as I know. When I was talking with her, she just gave me some information about Remi and Summer, which is why I spoke with Remi. She said they'd had some huge falling out. She wasn't sure why."

Meadow raised her eyebrows. "Well, that's very interesting that she called Remi out. That was probably because she was trying to divert attention from herself."

"From herself? Did Tobi have a reason to want to harm Summer?"

"Absolutely! Her husband was having an affair with Summer."

Beatrice apparently looked so stunned by this information that Meadow chuckled. "I forget that you're not as much into the gossip circuit as I am."

"Does everyone know about the affair? Poor Tobi."

"I don't think everyone knew, but I found out about it, so I'm guessing at least a few people know. I forget who told me, but it was someone in the quilting guild. She'd spotted Quinn and Summer canoodling together somewhere in town."

"Gracious." Beatrice decided that was plenty of reason for Tobi to have been unhappy with Summer, as witnessed by Mellie.

Meadow continued, "So Tobi had plenty of reason to want to implicate someone else. What did you find out from Remi? And where did you catch up with her?"

"Oh, I needed to get a new book from the library. Of course, I used the opportunity to have a conversation with Remi. Luckily, the library was pretty quiet at the time. She told me that she did have an issue with Summer, but she shrugged it off as something unimportant to her now."

Meadow vigorously nodded. "I'm sure she did! Wouldn't you? What was her issue with Summer?"

"Remi said she'd had a crush on Quinn before he became involved with Tobi. He apparently is quite a reader, and they'd talk about books when he was in there."

Meadow smiled. "Considering how Quinn looks, I have the feeling Remi was interested in more than just his mind."

"I've no doubt. Anyway, Remi was shy about approaching Quinn and I guess wanted to make sure she wasn't going to humiliate herself by trying to get a date with him if he wasn't at all interested. Summer knew Quinn because he'd once been her neighbor, and she offered to find out if Quinn might be amenable to going out with Remi."

Meadow's eyes were big. "This sounds like a storyline off that soap opera I used to watch."

"It sounds like something from elementary school to me, but I can understand Remi being a bit shy. Anyway, Summer never asked Quinn."

"What?"

Beatrice said, "That's right. At least, that's what Remi surmises. Summer claimed that she *had* asked Quinn and that he said he was just interested in Remi as a friend. But then, the next time Quinn came into the library, he acted as if nothing had changed between them. Remi thought that he might be acting at least slightly awkward if Summer had really questioned him about dating her. Instead, he was still flirty with her."

"So why didn't she just ask him out right then?"

"Well, I guess part of her wondered if Summer *had* asked him. Then Remi would look pretty desperate. I suppose she just wanted to leave the ball in his court. Unfortunately, soon afterward, Quinn started dating Tobi," said Beatrice.

"His now-wife," said Meadow. "This does indeed sound quite a lot like my soap opera! Except, on the show, the man ends up being abducted by aliens. So then he doesn't get to be with *either* of the women."

As Meadow prattled on about alien abductions, the treachery of so-called female friends, and other things from her soap opera, Boris grinned earnestly at Beatrice as if pointing out what a very good boy he was being. Beatrice obligingly gave him a treat. And, since Noo-noo looked a bit miffed at this, she gave the corgi one, too.

Meadow finally wrapped up her narrative about the show and said, "So is the thinking that Remi killed Summer because Summer lied to her?"

Beatrice shrugged. "It seems pretty far-fetched, doesn't it?"

"I'm sure Ramsay wouldn't think much of it as a motive. But then, he's not much of a romantic."

Beatrice lifted an eyebrow. "Really? With all that poetry writing?"

Meadow smiled. "Okay. Well, sometimes he writes me poetry. But I still don't think he'd consider Remi to have much of a motive for murder."

"I totally agree. It's just that Remi and Summer were seen to have a falling-out. And the falling-out was apparently over Quinn."

Meadow said, "Do you know who you're going to speak with next?"

"I'm thinking I need to speak with Danica. Remi said that Summer somehow got Danica fired from her job. She worked with her at the fitness center in Lenoir. After she was fired, Danica has been working as a waitress. She's had trouble finding a job in fitness."

Meadow made a face. "Summer sounds like a monster."

"I don't know if I'd go that far."

Meadow said, "But really! I think she was. There's a common theme here: Summer wrecking people's lives on purpose. I think she must have gotten a kick out of it. She messed up Remi's chances with Quinn, she got Danica fired, and she made Harlowe quit his job to help her at hers."

"It sounded like Harlowe cheerfully gave up his job at the store to give Summer a hand," offered Beatrice.

Meadow, however, was beyond listening. "Here's the thing—she made the wrong person mad. Like we were saying, none of these are really major motives. But they could have been the straws that broke the camel's back. Somebody got fed up with Summer's shenanigans and decided to get rid of her once and for all." She paused. "Do you know Danica well?"

Beatrice shook her head. "I don't really know her at all. Piper knows her, though, from around town. Piper said she'd have preferred to take fitness classes with Danica because Summer was something of a health zealot. The only reason Remi knew about Danica being fired is because Danica was in the library trying to use their job resources to find work." Now that she said it, she thought it was odd Remi had even told her about Danica. She knew the library was one of those places that made a point of respecting patrons' privacy. Perhaps it was a sign of how indignant Remi was at Summer that she mentioned it.

Meadow snorted. "Awful. That Summer was a menace."

Boris, a milder menace, had stealthily crept closer to the treats that Beatrice had put on the table. Before she knew what happened, he jumped up, put his front paws on the table, and gobbled up the remaining treats before giving Beatrice an apologetic grin. Noo-noo shot him a chilly, peeved look.

Meadow frowned. "Now, Boris! That wasn't very nice. I'm not even altogether sure that you deserved those treats."

Beatrice was quite sure he hadn't.

Meadow stood up. "I suppose Boris and I should be getting home and leave you and Noo-noo to relax. I've got some tidying up I've got to do before I start in with cooking supper. What are you making for supper tonight?"

"Something special. Grilled cheese sandwiches," said Beatrice with a smile.

Meadow raised an eyebrow. "Ramsay would think I'd had a small stroke if I put that out for supper. The thing is, I guess, is that I enjoy cooking and you don't really seem to."

"I actively dislike cooking, as a matter of fact. I didn't do much of it when I was working in Atlanta, since it was just me . . . I guess I fell out of the habit. When Piper was little, I did make an effort, but as soon as she went away to college, I was pretty much done with it. Wyatt likes cooking pretty well, though. And he's good at it."

Meadow said, "You're lucky. If Ramsay were in charge of our food, grilled cheese would seem like a luxury food. We'd be eating cereal every night." She whistled to Boris, who carefully ignored her, instead chasing a bumblebee that had made its presence known. Meadow whistled again and Boris, shooting her a look, reluctantly walked over.

"We'll see you later. Remember the guild meeting is tomorrow! You've had so much going on lately, I worried you might forget about it."

Beatrice had, if only for a couple of hours. But she quickly said, "You know I couldn't forget about quilting."

Meadow and Boris took their leave. Noo-noo looked somewhat relieved and Beatrice reached over to rub the little dog. "It's nice and quiet now, isn't it? I suppose I really need to put some time into finishing Piper's UFO. Or I could think more about what I should serve with the grilled cheese sandwich entrée tonight. Fruit with the grilled cheese? Salad with it?"

Noo-noo seemed to think that both fruit and salad would be nice. And, perhaps, a place at the table just for her.

As Beatrice was mulling over the somewhat limited choices, her phone rang. "Hi there, Piper."

"Hi, Mama. Will has a little extra energy and I'm restless, too. Must be the fact that I never got that exercise class in. I think we're going to head to the playground at the park and get some of his ya-yas out. Want to join us?"

Beatrice certainly did. Not only was she always eager to get a visit in with her daughter and grandson, it meant an end to her overthinking supper plans. "I'll meet you there in a few minutes."

She carefully wrote a note to Wyatt telling him *not* to make supper—that she was making grilled cheese when she got home. Then she got into her car and headed off to the park.

Chapter Eight

The park was one of her favorite spots in Dappled Hills. It was right in the middle of downtown and had playgrounds for both toddlers and older kids. A walking path curved through the park, connecting to an extensive greenway used by joggers and bicyclists. There was also a trail leading up a mountain at the far end for the days when more rigorous exercise would be desired.

Piper had already arrived, and she and Will waved as Beatrice hurried up to join them. Will pointed to the slide and said to Beatrice, "I slide, Grandmama."

Beatrice and Piper looked at each other with wide eyes. Although Will had been taking stabs at Beatrice's grandmother name for some time, he hadn't been able to master it until just then.

Beatrice gave him a cuddle. "You slide? On that big kid slide?"

Will gave her an adorable grin and made a little happy dance.

Piper said, "He wants to give it a go. I figured it's kind of a transition slide between the little kid one and the very biggest one. If you can hold his hand while he comes down, I can spot him on the stairs."

Sure enough, Will went right up the stairs with no problem. The slide was short enough that Beatrice could hold Will's hand from the ground as he ecstatically slid down, arms held up as he went, like he was on a roller coaster. He was so proud of himself as Piper and Beatrice cheered for him afterward. He grinned at them.

Will, naturally, wanted to go down the slide again. And then he went down again, and again, and again as if he wanted to master his new skill.

Beatrice wondered at one point if he were tiring at all. *She* was getting tired, and she was only holding on to his hand. Finally, Piper told Will it was time for a snack and rest.

"I brought snacks for us, too, Mama," said Piper with a grin.

"That's smart of you. I must be out of practice because it didn't even occur to me."

Piper said, "I keep a backpack by the door to remind me to get waters and snacks."

They sat down at a picnic table. Beatrice gave Will his sippy cup as Piper dispersed apple slices and graham crackers.

After a few minutes, Piper said quietly to Beatrice, "I see Danica over there. She was looking over in our direction and then she looked away. Let's try to have her join us."

Beatrice nodded. She was interested in speaking with Danica, anyway.

Piper waved to Danica, and Danica couldn't avoid coming over. She was wearing her running clothes and shoes and looked as if she was just taking a break from a jog. Her long brown hair was pulled back in a ponytail. She smiled uncertainly at Piper and Beatrice. "How are y'all doing today?" Then she gave Will a bigger smile. "Wow, you've gotten so big, Will!"

Will gave her a big grin before focusing his attention back on his apple slice.

"Would you like to join us, Danica? I went a little crazy with the apple slices, and we have far more than we need. I think I get into a rhythm when I start slicing and just don't stop. Do you know my mom?"

Beatrice introduced herself, and Danica smiled at her. She said, "I'm not hungry, but I'd like to sit with you for a few minutes. I took a run and pushed myself a little more than I usually do."

Danica took a seat next to Will, and he watched her with big eyes while he snacked.

"I haven't seen you around for a while," said Piper. "How have you been doing?"

To Beatrice's and Piper's dismay, Danica burst heartily into tears.

Piper quickly dug in her diaper bag and pulled out a pack of tissues. She thrust them into Danica's hand. "I'm so sorry! I didn't mean to upset you."

Danica wiped her eyes and then gave a short laugh. "It's not you, it's me. Everything seems to make me cry these days." She regained control of her emotions and then added, "You wouldn't have known, but I lost my job over at the fitness center months ago. And I can't seem to find another one. I've been waitressing and things like that, but I've been looking nonstop for another job in fitness. I just feel . . . lost. I had a whole routine that was centered around my work and now that it's gone, I don't really know what to do with all the hours in the day. That's why I'm out here for a jog."

Piper said slowly, "I'm really sorry to hear that. It must be so unsettling to lose your routine like that. What kinds of places have you been looking? Just dedicated fitness centers, or other places, too?"

"Fitness centers and places that have fitness classes. So churches and places like that, too. But the classes at churches seem to be volunteer-led for the most part. And the fitness centers are fully staffed right now."

"Have you thought about the schools? I have lots of contacts in the school district. I could recommend you for a physical education job at the high school. They just lost someone there who relocated."

Danica looked wistful. "I'd love that job, Piper, but I just don't know how the district would take the fact that I got fired from my last job. I think they would think that was a major mark against me."

Piper said, "What happened, if you don't mind my asking?"

Danica rubbed her head as if it hurt. "I got on the wrong side of Summer is what happened. I know I should have kept my cool, but she'd been provoking me for weeks and I finally snapped. I'd been amazingly patient with her up until then. I should have known better."

"What kind of provocation?" asked Beatrice.

"Well, the final straw was when I developed this new fitness program and she took credit for it. Once I'd found out about that, I saw red. I lunged at her and shoved her so hard that she stumbled backwards and fell over, hitting her head on the window ledge. It really wasn't anything, but Summer played it up to management. She made it sound as if I'd assaulted her."

Piper winced.

"I know," said Danica, seeing her reaction. "Obviously, the fitness center thought I might be a risk if they kept me on. What I hated was seeing Summer's smug reaction when they fired me. The thing was, I'd been working there for a while and I knew I couldn't get a good recommendation letter from management. I mean, I was the one who got *Summer* the job there—I'd been working there longer. But, without a recommendation letter, I've been looking for a job ever since. And it's been a while."

Beatrice considered this for a minute. "Were the police involved? I mean, were they called out during the altercation with Summer or after it?"

Danica shook her head. "No way. Like I said, it wasn't even that big of a deal. Summer pushed my buttons, I shoved her, she fell. That was it. It wasn't a police matter."

"Then the police would have no record of it or you. I'd think it wouldn't be a problem getting a job with the school district," said Beatrice.

Danica looked a little more cheerful. "That's true. I didn't think about that. The whole thing has just been so humiliating. I can't believe I let myself be provoked like that. I promise I'm usually a very even-tempered person."

Piper said, "Well, it definitely doesn't sound as if Summer was behaving herself."

"Nope. Will is much better-behaved than she was."

Will, spotting his name during the otherwise inexplicable conversation, gave them a grin that showed off his new little teeth.

Danica ruffled the boy's hair and said, "I've been trying to get over all of my negative feelings about the whole episode, though. After all, it's forcing me to look into new places to work. It's good for me to expand my horizons a little and think outside the box. The fitness center in Lenoir was pretty stressful, after all, and dealing with stress is totally counterproductive. I mean, the big thing about working in the fitness industry is a focus on health. We're expected to eat healthy, hydrate, and work out. Living with daily stress, like I was, is just about the worst thing you can do for your health."

Beatrice said, "And Summer was mainly the cause of your stress there? It seems to me that Summer had a hard time getting along with people."

"She could be tough to get along with, for sure. And you're right—Summer was the cause of most of my stress over there. Maybe the management was the cause of a tiny bit of it. Anyway, you'd never guess it, but people loved Summer as a fitness instructor. She could tailor exercises for the group on the fly. Someone could tell her that his back was hurting, and she'd throw in modifications for everything she was doing. She was very knowledgeable. Plus, she was always encouraging and supportive; pretty much exactly the opposite of how she was with others. There was always that intensity in the background, though. It was hard to be around her for very long."

Piper said, "Do you have any ideas as to who might have done this to her?"

"I've been thinking about it a lot. There were quite a few people who got on her bad side. I heard around town that she'd been upset with her contractor, who was working on her studio. Dan, I think his name is."

Beatrice immediately said, "We actually know Dan Whitner and can vouch that he's a great guy and an excellent contractor. We can't imagine him doing anything to harm Summer or anyone else."

Piper added, "He does amazing work and can make or fix just about anything."

"I can believe that," said Danica. "Summer always did have unreasonable expectations about everything. She was a real perfectionist."

"I gather that her project wasn't the only one Dan was working on at the time. That might have made Summer upset," said Beatrice.

Danica snorted. "Of course it would have. Summer always had to come first and her studio was her pet project. If Dan isn't the one responsible for her death, I'm thinking it must have been her husband—Harlowe. He's the obvious candidate. The husbands are always responsible, aren't they?"

"Well, I think they're usually the prime suspects," said Beatrice.

"Living with Summer must have been a nightmare. Plus, she was always pushing him around—I noticed that when I was working with her."

Piper's eyes were big. "Like physically?"

Danica said, "Metaphorically, but it *could* have been physical, too. Summer was a powerful woman. I'd hear her on the phone talking with Harlowe and she'd tell him that he couldn't spend money on something he wanted to purchase because she had more money than he did."

"I can't imagine that went over well," said Beatrice dryly.

"I don't know what he said on the other end of the line, but I'm sure he wasn't happy about it. Plus, Summer wasn't always the most faithful of wives."

Beatrice and Piper both opened their eyes wide in surprise, and Danica nodded. "I'd see her flirting with male clients all the time. She'd even go out to dinner with them sometimes. She was in Lenoir, of course, so Harlowe would have just thought she had a late class."

Beatrice was starting to feel sorry for Harlowe.

Danica looked at her watch. "Anyway, I should get on with my exercise, especially if I'm going to keep on applying for jobs. I've got to make sure I stay in shape."

Piper said, "If you send me your contact info, I can email you the information about the position at the high school."

Danica quickly texted it to Piper, thanked her, then took her leave. Piper threw away their trash, and they settled Will on the swings. "What did you make of all that?" asked Piper as she pushed Will.

Beatrice watched with a faint smile as Will's wispy hair blew back and forth as he swung. "I think Summer could be a very difficult woman."

"I know. Danica, of course, had good reason to get rid of her. I mean, Summer really messed up her job chances. The high school will likely ask her why she doesn't have a recommendation letter from her previous employer. I can imagine Danica would feel like taking some revenge on Summer. After all, she was mad enough at her to give her a shove. But I just can't picture her murdering her, just the same."

"You were nice to give her a job lead. There just aren't a lot of fitness jobs in this neck of the woods."

Piper shrugged. "She's a friend of mine, even if we don't really do much together now that Will is here. It wasn't fair, what happened to her."

They watched Will, and both chuckled as he lifted his face upward, enjoying the breeze and the sun on his skin.

"He's a happy guy. Thanks for inviting me to join you," said Beatrice.

After another thirty minutes of swinging, sandbox play, and the slide again, Will's energy level was finally starting to flag. It was a good thing, because so was Beatrice's.

"We'd better head back home before things go downhill," said Piper wryly.

Beatrice gave them both a hug. "It's always good to leave the party when you're still having fun."

"And toddler moods can turn on a dime. Thanks for joining us, Mama."

Beatrice drove back home to get started on the grilled cheeses and whatever accompanying dish she could figure out. She was still mulling between the fruit and the salad. When she drove up to the house, though, she saw Wyatt's car was already there.

And, as she walked inside, there was a delicious aroma wafting through the air.

"I hope you didn't cook. I left you a note that I was going to make grilled cheeses," said Beatrice, feeling a little guilty. She hadn't intended Wyatt to cook anything after having worked all day.

"I thought I'd pick up some food for us," said Wyatt with a grin. He handed Beatrice a plate and stood back so that she could see the assorted Chinese food in front of him. "We haven't had takeout for a while and I thought this might be a good day for it."

"And how! I've been strangely reluctant to cook anything today. I was just squaring my shoulders and going to whip out the sandwiches and some fruit or something. I'm glad you had a better plan."

They sat down at the table together with Noo-noo close by and attentive in case any morsels slipped away from them.

"How did your day go?" asked Wyatt.

Beatrice swallowed down a bite of her egg roll and said, "It was pretty good, actually." She recounted her trip to the library to see Remi and the visit with Danica in the park with Piper and Will.

She summed up, "It seems as if Summer was deliberately messing with people's lives."

Wyatt sighed. "It does sound like she could be manipulative. Is that what you're thinking? That she pushed the wrong person too far?"

"I think so. I need to fill Ramsay in on what I've found out."

Wyatt nodded. "That's a good idea. I worry about you when you have a lot of information like this. Worry that someone might be desperate to keep that information from coming out."

"Maybe I can give him a quick call tomorrow. Or even leave him a voice mail." She had the feeling that Wyatt, sweetly concerned about her, would rather her fill in Ramsay now. But whether it was the busy day or the activity at the park, Beatrice felt in dire need of a quiet evening with her book, husband, and dog.

Fortunately, that was precisely what Wyatt wanted, too. And so Wyatt played jazz music softly in the background as Beatrice curled up on the sofa with Noo-noo, and Wyatt and Beatrice read their books.

Chapter Nine

The next morning was the guild meeting. Fortunately, it was late in the morning, so Beatrice had some time to do a bit of last-minute, frantic quilting in order to finish Piper's UFO. Despite her rush at the eleventh hour, she had to admit the quilt had turned out surprisingly well. It was something she wasn't going to be reluctant to show off at the meeting.

After taking Noo-noo for a walk and having a late breakfast, Beatrice headed over to the quilt shop, which was where this month's meeting was being held. As she walked in with her quilt, she could hear Tiggy inside, speaking with a bit of agitation in her voice. This wasn't in itself unusual, since Tiggy could get indignant over any number of things. Sugary cereal was a recent target, Beatrice remembered.

As she got closer, however, she realized that Tiggy seemed to be speaking about Dan Whitner, her paramour. And, instead of being merely indignant, she was nearly tearful.

Meadow was with her and seemed to be in about the same state. On spotting Beatrice, she waved her over. "Tell Beatrice, Tiggy."

So Tiggy, scrubbing a stray tear off her face, said, "Oh, it's just awful, Beatrice. Poor Dan. Summer's slander was already affecting his business. She was telling everyone that he was doing a poor job with her studio construction. Can you imagine?"

Beatrice shook her head. "Dan always does a great job with everything he takes on."

"Exactly! But Summer was going around telling everyone that he wasn't. That was bad enough. Now, people seem to think he's a suspect and that he murdered Summer." More tears slid down Tiggy's face.

Meadow was incensed. "Dan is a perfectly wonderful contractor. Anyone would be lucky to have his help with their projects. Tell Beatrice what you were telling me about Dan's health."

"Is the stress affecting his health?" asked Beatrice, frowning.

"Worse than that," said Tiggy with a shaky sigh. "He needs to have an expensive surgery done. The timing of this is just awful. Because he's self-employed, he doesn't have very good insurance. And with his business having fallen off with Summer's slander?" She shook her head.

Meadow said, "Beatrice, we've got to find out who killed Summer, so Dan won't be a suspect anymore."

Dan, having heard his name, suddenly joined them. He was a gentle, quiet man who worked hard and was always very responsible with his projects. It was one reason Beatrice felt bad for him—he definitely didn't deserve what Summer had said about him. He gave them a smile, but there was hurt in his eyes. "Thanks so much, ladies. It's been a hard time, for sure."

Meadow said, "I'm just sorry this is happening. Ramsay hasn't been questioning you, has he?" Her tone boded ill for her police chief husband.

Dan smiled and said, "Of course he has, Meadow. That's his job. People have probably told him what Summer said about me. After all, it would look to the police as if I have a motive."

Meadow gave an indignant huff. "Well, I hope you set them straight. Did you have a good alibi for Summer's death?"

Dan looked regretful. "Didn't know I needed one. I'd been out walking my dog early. The dog can't give much of an alibi."

"What did you make of Summer?" asked Beatrice. "I'm only asking because it seems as if she had a tough time getting along with others."

"I didn't really know her very well . . . you know, I only knew her from working for her."

Meadow said, "But you must have picked up some sort of impression of her. If we know more about what she was like or who she might have had issues with, maybe we can figure out who did this."

Dan nodded and then reluctantly said, "She was pretty hot-tempered. One minute she'd be as cool as a cucumber and the next she was fighting mad because I told her putting a second coat of paint on would have to wait until I finished another job."

"It sounds like the problem was Summer and not you," said Beatrice dryly.

Dan said, "Well, she was kind of a perfectionist. I can't blame her—she was spending a lot of money to make this studio. She kept saying it was her dream to create the place. Summer wanted everything just so."

"And you were the perfect person to do the job," said Meadow hotly.

"That wasn't really the issue. The problem was that she didn't seem to understand that I had other jobs to handle. I'm not some big company with a lot of subcontractors; it's just me. She wanted me to work a hundred percent on her project. Plus, she didn't understand that sometimes things run behind schedule, for lots of different reasons. Summer wanted it to run either completely on time or even ahead of schedule."

"It sounds like she was very pushy," said Beatrice.

"Very. But, there again, I sort of understood, even though I thought she was being unreasonable. After all, she wanted to open up her studio and start having clients and classes and some income. It made me sad when I heard she was gone. She had this big dream and she never even got to have a single class at her studio."

"That's very generous of you to feel sorry for Summer," said Beatrice. "Like Meadow mentioned, it could be helpful for us to know who might have had problems with Summer. Did you overhear any arguments or sense any tension between Summer and someone else?"

Dan thought about the question. Then he said slowly, "I guess you could say her husband. But I know lots of folks have tension in their marriage."

Tiggy's eyes were big. "They say it's always the husband, don't they?"

Dan quickly added, "I'm not going to say he did it. But Summer was putting him down all the time. Making him feel bad about his job and then making him feel bad about not having one."

"But he *did* have a job. He was working for Summer and trying to help her start up her business," said Meadow indignantly. "He was being supportive."

Dan shrugged. "Maybe sometimes Summer liked having him around and they got along great. I just didn't see those times."

Tiggy said, "I hate the fact that somebody else did this and is letting Dan take all the blame."

"People are actually *saying* that Dan did it? Out loud, I mean?" Meadow looked aghast.

"They might or might not be. I'm not sure," said Tiggy. "But the fact of the matter is that Dan isn't getting as many jobs as he used to. That tells me they're thinking he's involved somehow, right?"

Beatrice said, "I'm sure Ramsay will find out who's behind this soon, Dan. In the meantime, we'll keep our eyes and ears open. Whatever we hear, we'll pass along to Ramsay."

Dan looked relieved. "Thank you, Beatrice. Now, I'd better head out. I understand you're all about to have a quilt meeting here."

And indeed, the guild members had been filing in with their quilts and heading toward the back room where Posy had set everything up for the guild meeting. Dan collected his things and left.

"Are you joining us today?" Meadow asked Tiggy.

Beatrice thought Meadow looked a little apprehensive as to the answer she might get. Tiggy, as much as she loved crafting, was not the most adept. Savannah and Georgia were most relieved that she'd given up dressmaking, considering they'd been wearing her poorly crafted matching dresses for some time. Meadow had expressed fervent hopes that Tiggy might stick with some other craft besides quilting.

Tiggy said, "Oh no, I think I should head out myself. I'm going to keep working on a dress I'm making for myself. Something special for when Dan and I hit the town." She frowned.

"If we *can* hit the town, what with Dan's lack of funds. Unfortunately, I'm not that flush with cash either."

"Don't you worry about a thing," said Meadow stoutly. "We're on it, aren't we Beatrice?"

Beatrice gave Tiggy a reassuring smile. "We'll do everything we can to help."

As Tiggy took her leave, Beatrice and Meadow joined the others in the back room. Posy had made sure the plain space was decorated with quilts and had opened one of the windows to let in the breeze. She'd also put out a nice spread of food, which the quilters were already enjoying. Beatrice helped herself to some berries, brie, and crackers.

"A very French-looking snack," said fellow quilter Georgia with her gentle smile.

Beatrice smiled back at her. She'd always liked Georgia and her sister, Savannah. They'd been "the Potter sisters" before Georgia married Tony. Savannah, quite stuck in her ways, had something of a tough adjustment after the wedding. Now, though, Savannah had found her own direction. She was glad Savannah was happy because it made Georgia so much less-stressed.

Beatrice said, "I'm trying to stick with some healthier things after I felt my waistband getting a little tighter. Although I'd love to dive into that pile of chocolate chip cookies that Posy put out."

"I think you'll have to fight Miss Sissy for them," said Georgia with a laugh.

Sure enough, the old lady seemed to have laid claim to the cookies, giving anyone who got close to them the side eye.

Georgia said, "Were you able to finish up the UFO you were assigned? I know you're usually super-busy with your grandson. I don't remember who your UFO was for."

"Will is an excellent and very cuddly excuse for anything that I don't want to do," said Beatrice wryly. "But since my unfinished project assignment was one of Piper's quilts, I figured I'd better get on it. I finished by the skin of my teeth."

Posy stood at the front of the room, gently calling the meeting to order. Everyone sat down in the folding chairs at the long table Posy had set up before the meeting. She smiled at them all. "I hope everyone had fun with the UFO project. I'm excited to see my unfinished object finished! Before we reveal our finished quilts, Meadow has a quick announcement she asked me to make."

Meadow was still looking flushed from their conversation with Dan and Tiggy. "Hey everybody. As you know, Tiggy is Savannah and Georgia's aunt and Dan, her beau, is a friend of the guild and has done a lot of work for most of us. I've heard through the grapevine that he's got to have a very expensive surgery at a time where he might be financially pinched. I'd like to propose a fundraiser to help him out."

There was a general murmur of support from the room, and Meadow beamed at them. "I thought you'd feel that way. The only problem is, because it's medically related, time is of the essence. Now, I'm pretty sure the library will let us use their community room if we ask. I'm thinking about a silent auction for some of our quilts. I know the library has let us put flyers at their checkout desk before. What do you think?"

Georgia called out, "This is really sweet of everybody. Thanks, y'all. It's been a real worry of Tiggy's."

Meadow said, "We'll see what we can do. Knowing Dan, I was thinking it might be best if we keep the fact we're doing the event for him as a surprise. Better to have it be a done deal so he can't try to persuade us not to help him out. That's all I had to say. Can't wait to see everyone's UFOs!"

Everyone applauded and then Posy covered some other guild business as Piper came in with Will and sat next to Beatrice. She whispered, "Running a little behind today."

"I'll fill you in on what you've missed later," said Beatrice with a smile.

Will's eyes danced as he looked at Beatrice. "Gran-mama."

Beatrice felt her heart swell as she gave the little boy a cuddle.

Finally, it was time for everyone to unveil the quilts. They all looked really nice, of course, but the main point was that they were *finished*. They weren't languishing in a craft room or a closet. And everyone was delighted to see their projects finally done.

Meadow whispered to Beatrice, "Savannah's standing up. I can't wait to see what she did with my UFO."

Savannah cleared her throat and looked around the room severely. "First off, I think this was the most challenging quilt I've ever worked on."

There was a murmur around the room. Savannah was a very accomplished quilter. Her quilts were always completely perfect, with no bad stitching.

Savannah said, "When Meadow gave me her crazy quilt to finish, I believe my mind was well and truly blown. I usually like to impose order on everything in my world."

Beatrice thought about Savannah's small home and how absolutely everything that came into it had a place. And, if it didn't, how Savannah would either give the item away or throw it away.

Savannah took a deep breath. "Anyway, I have a confession to make. Part of me wanted to rip out what Meadow had completed and start over, making all the bits and pieces very organized and systematic."

Meadow started chuckling. "That must have put you in a real quandary, Savannah."

Savannah gave her a weary look. "I had to battle my inner demons."

"I wouldn't have cared at all. You could have done it, and the quilt probably would have looked much better than it did before," said Meadow.

"But no, I overcame my baser instincts," said Savannah proudly. "And I feel really good about the fact that I worked within the guild's guidelines for the project."

Posy said quickly, "We wouldn't have had a problem with you going off in your own direction."

But Savannah shook her head. "I should follow the rules, just the same as anybody else. And now, here's the finished product."

It looked marvelous. Meadow started clapping her hands when she saw it. You could definitely tell, however, which part was Meadow's and which part was Savannah's. Meadow's section of the crazy quilt was very abstract, with bits and pieces of fabric in different colors and shapes all over the base. Savannah, however, had neatly trimmed her fabric stash bits into right triangles. The effect was of a crazy quilt that had been somewhat tamed halfway through the process.

Piper gave Beatrice a hug after she showed off Piper's finished quilt.

"I'm *so* happy to see it finished. Thanks, Mama!"

Somehow, Piper had managed to find the time to finish Beatrice's, as well. She'd not only finished it, but she'd done an amazing job with the log cabin design.

Beatrice said, "I love the quilt you finished for me, too."

Piper chuckled. "It was easy enough. I'm not sure why it went into the UFO pile at your house."

Beatrice sighed. "I remember exactly what happened. I'd picked out the traditional design on purpose and was having a good time working on it. But then Posy hosted a workshop on something more contemporary and I put the quilt aside to work on something else. I seem to be more easily distracted these days than I used to be. Anyway, now I feel more inspired to finish some of the UFOs in my pile instead of rushing on to the next new project."

Meadow asked the group if finishing the UFOs was hard, and everyone shook their heads. Georgia said with a laugh, "It's because they weren't *our* unfinished projects, they were someone else's."

Posy said, "Isn't that the truth? I was on the point of using my UFO as backing for another quilt. I'm so glad I didn't now."

The different patterns, colors, and textures of the quilts always gave Beatrice a jolt of inspiration. Seeing what other people were doing made her want to get back home and get going with her quilting.

Posy said, "Now for some extra added motivation and inspiration, let's hear what everyone is planning on working on next."

Meadow said ruefully, "See, this is why I end up with UFOs. I'll start a perfectly good project with nice fabric and cute colors. I'll be totally dedicated to the quilt and have a complete vision for what I want it to look like. Then, the next thing I know, I listen to everybody saying what *they're* working on and suddenly I don't want to work on my perfectly good quilt any longer."

Georgia chuckled. "Yes, I'm the same way. It's like I'm distracted by everybody else's cool ideas."

Her sister, Savannah, said with a frown, "Really? That's never happened to me before."

"That's because you're always good at keeping to a schedule," said Meadow with a laugh. "I want to be like Savannah when I grow up."

They went around the room and took turns saying what they were tackling next. Piper said, "I'm taking it a little easy now and doing a mug rug."

Savannah frowned again. "A mug rug? What's that?"

"Oh, it's a quilted mat. It's just big enough to serve as a coaster for a drink and a small snack. Here, I have a picture on my phone of one I did recently."

Piper handed her phone to Savannah, who peered at it. The one Piper had finished had a blue polka-dotted border, and small squares of blueberries, a pinwheel, and stripes in shades of blue.

"That's kind of cute," said Savannah in a mulling type of tone.

Meadow blinked in amazement at the idea of Savannah branching from her beloved geometric patterns. "Are you going to try making one?"

"Maybe. But mine would be a checkerboard with white and black," said Savannah.

Beatrice hid a smile. She loved the way Savannah imposed order on her universe.

June Bug put up her hand shyly.

Posy beamed at her. "What are you working on, June Bug?"

The little woman stood up and said, "A checkerboard, too." She gave Savannah a small smile. "But for playing checkers. You can buy jumbo-sized checkers online. Making it for Katie."

June Bug's niece Katie lived with her and seemed to have a very happy existence under June Bug's thoughtful care.

"That might be fun for Will," said Beatrice to Piper.

She laughed. "I know you and Meadow think Will is brilliant, Mama, but the fact is that he's just a toddler. I don't think he's quite ready for checkers yet, unless it's chewing on them. Maybe you could make it and save it for later."

By the end of everyone's project reports, Beatrice felt even more inspired than she'd been with the UFOs. She reminded herself that she should take her new inspiration and use it to deplete her fabric stash and maybe tackle one of her own UFOs again. There were a couple of quilts that just needed backing and would be easy enough to finish.

"You've got that determined look on your face," said Piper.

Beatrice said, "I'm trying to resist the temptation to start something new. Like Meadow said, that's where I get into trouble. It's like there's a shiny new object and it pulls me off in another direction. Maybe I need to organize all the projects and fabric I have. A spreadsheet would be a good way to do it."

Piper looked doubtful. "Would it? It seems like it could be a good way of spending a lot of time tweaking the spreadsheet and less time with actual quilting."

"True. And I do tend to get carried away, as you can imagine. But I do love a good spreadsheet. I remember when I was working at the museum, I felt like I could really keep track of all the hundreds of exhibits so easily with a simple inventory. We'd lend out exhibits to other museums, and it helped so much. I don't have as much stuff at home, of course—the fact that Wyatt and I reside in a tiny cabin really helps my stash from getting out of control. But I feel like I'm not even totally sure *what* I have in my fabric collection. If I noted each one that I have and write a short description of the pattern, I think it would really help."

Will had been listening to his grandmother intently in Piper's arms. He couldn't have known what she was talking about, but a big grin spread across his face as if he just enjoyed listening to her voice and having one of his favorite people nearby.

After the meeting, everyone helped themselves to more food and catching up. Maisie, the shop cat, had padded curiously into the back room to see what everyone was up to. Then she'd happily curled up in Savannah's lap, purring loudly.

Beatrice walked over to her. "Looks like you're stuck."

Savannah cuddled the cat. "It's worth it. Of course, when I go back home, Smoke is going to think I've been cheating on him with another cat."

"Can I get you a plate of food or some water?"

"I think I'm all right. Thanks, though." She paused. "I heard from Piper that you were the one who found Summer."

Beatrice pulled up a chair and sat next to her. "I'm afraid so."

Savannah said, "I was kind of confused. Not about the murder, but about who she was married to. Piper was saying she was married to the manager at the grocery store. But I'd seen her with someone else who was definitely not the grocery manager."

"Was it Quinn?" Beatrice remembered her conversation with Meadow. She'd said that someone in the guild had spotted Quinn and Summer together.

Savannah brightened. "That's his name, yes. Quinn. I'd thought he was married to that woman who is always volunteering at church, but then I figured I'd gotten it wrong."

"No, I'm afraid you got it right. Tobi is from church. I understand that Quinn and Summer might have been seeing each other."

Savannah raised an eyebrow. "Well, they weren't being very secret about it. That's why I thought they were the ones who were married. Summer was acting like she had every right to be with him."

Beatrice was about to respond, but Savannah lost interest in the conversation. "Piper and Will are coming over," she said with a big smile.

Will was everyone's favorite part of guild meetings. He didn't always come with Piper, so when he did, it was a treat. He was always very good and would spend the meeting munching on a cookie and taking in all the colors and textures of the quilts surrounding him. This time, Piper had brought some cardboard lacing cards with her. The cards had pictures of farm animals on them and the idea was that Will could lace the shoelaces through the cards as if he were sewing along with the group.

Piper said, "Will wondered if he could say hi to Maisie. And you, too, Savannah."

Will grinned at Savannah, who smiled back at him. "Would you like to see Maisie, Will?"

The little boy gently rubbed the cat as he and Savannah had a little chat.

Beatrice said to Piper, "How did you manage to get Will away from Miss Sissy? She usually tends to hog him whenever she sees him."

Piper chuckled. "I think this time she was more preoccupied with the food table. Posy put out some especially appealing treats this time. Meadow is probably the one we have to worry about. I saw her eyeing Will a couple of minutes ago." She turned more serious and said, "How are you doing, by the way, Mama? Finding Summer was pretty dramatic. Have you been sleeping all right?"

"Well, I had a hard time at first. I did better last night. But I was thinking about you this morning and wondering if you'd figured out another way to exercise. You'd seemed really excited about going to Summer's studio."

Piper shook her head. "I mean, I know it's a minor point compared to poor Summer's death. But I was really looking for-ward to having some guided classes that were local to me. Right now, Dappled Hills doesn't have any really dedicated fitness programs. Of course there are classes at the church, but those don't always fit my schedule."

Beatrice said, "I wonder what Harlowe plans on doing with Summer's studio. It sounds like it was really going to fill a need here in town."

"I hope he's going to continue with it, but I totally understand if he doesn't. The whole place must hold very painful memories for him." Piper looked at her mother, noticing the lines of worry on her face. She quickly said, "On to better topics. I'm so excited that you finished that project of mine. I think it's going to cover that tired old hand-me-down chair in our living room."

Beatrice smiled at her. "To cover it up?"

"Well, let's say to *brighten* it up." Piper grinned back at her. "It's not that I don't really appreciate free furniture."

"If it were a cat, it definitely looks like it's at the end of its nine lives. The avocado green isn't particularly appealing, either."

Piper said, "I'd forgive the chair for its general unattractiveness if it were at least comfortable."

Beatrice chuckled. "I've had the misfortune of sitting in that chair before and know exactly what you mean. I think that's an excellent spot for the quilt. At any rate, it will make that corner more cheerful."

The quilters caught up with each other for a little while longer, and then the meeting broke up. Beatrice helped Posy get the room back in order and then headed home to take Noo-noo for a walk.

Chapter Ten

The walk ended up being a longer one than expected. When Beatrice had turned around to head back in the direction of the house, Noo-noo had stopped, looked at her, and pulled her forward. There was apparently a lovely smell coming from further down the road. After quite a bit longer, Noo-noo found the wondrous spot, explored it, and finally acquiesced to turning around for home.

Wyatt came home earlier than usual and Beatrice and Noo-noo arrived there right when he did. "What a pleasant surprise," said Beatrice, giving him a peck on the cheek.

Wyatt gave her a hug. "My meetings for the afternoon got cancelled. I thought we could do something fun."

"I'm all ears."

"Maybe get some ice cream downtown? I've been craving their peanut butter and chocolate fudge flavor. A little sugar might be just what I need to give me a pick-me-up today, too. I found myself nodding off at my desk."

"Ice cream would be perfect. And then maybe you and I could go to the store? You saved the day yesterday, but I think we're in the same fix for today, with nothing really appealing in the fridge."

And so the plan was set. Wyatt got two scoops of peanut butter and chocolate fudge in a cone and Beatrice went with her usual favorite of mint chocolate chip in a cup. She couldn't figure how Wyatt was able to eat his ice cream without it melting in the cone and getting all over him. But once again, he was completely spill-free as he finished his treat. Beatrice, on the other hand, had somehow managed to drip mint chocolate chip on herself, even with the cup.

"Should we head over to the grocery store?" asked Wyatt as they threw away their trash.

"Let's. And let's try not to make it like our last joint grocery shopping expedition."

Wyatt grinned at her. "You mean when we somehow purchased a hundred dollars' worth of groceries and had nothing to make a meal out of? I think we only do that when we're hungry."

"Well, we're certainly not hungry now, so let's avoid a repeat."

They drove the short distance to the grocery store and walked inside. Beatrice grimaced. "I really should have jotted down a list before we walked in. This is how I end up getting into trouble with impulse buys."

Wyatt said, "How about if I make a list while we start off in the produce area? We can't get into too much trouble there with impulse buying. Do you have paper and a pencil in your purse?"

Beatrice was quite sure she had pretty much everything anyone could possibly want in her purse, which was why it had been so impossibly heavy lately. She mentally put cleaning her purse out on her list of things to do. She handed him a small notepad and a pen.

Wyatt poised the pen over the notepad and thought. "Let's see. Healthy, easy meals." He pondered this for a while as Beatrice walked listlessly through the produce department, picking up various fruits and studying the vegetables.

"Any ideas?" she asked him. "I'm drawing a complete blank."

Wyatt said, "It's almost as if I can't remember what we eat on a day-to-day basis."

"Oh, believe me, I know. How about salads? We eat those sometimes."

Wyatt, however, didn't find the idea of a big salad for supper very appealing. "Maybe a *potato* and a salad?"

"Perhaps, if we're going for healthy, it should be a sweet potato and a salad."

Wyatt said, "That makes one meal."

"And a sort of pitiful one, at that. If we don't think of others, we're going to be in this exact same spot tomorrow, too."

They must have looked quite the picture, frowning into space. Edgenora, the church's excellent administrative assistant, said from behind them, "Are the two of you in some sort of trouble?"

They turned around, looking rueful. Beatrice said, "The sort of trouble where you can't think what you need to get at the store when you're already at the store."

"Can you throw out some supper ideas for us, Edgenora?" asked Wyatt with a wry grin. "You're so efficient that I have the feeling you have a sensible list with you."

Edgenora did indeed have a list. "Shredded chicken tacos, salmon pasta, honey chickpea bowls, and shrimp scampi with zucchini noodles."

Wyatt and Beatrice looked at each other. "Sensible, just as I mentioned," said Wyatt. He quickly jotted down the ideas Edgenora had given them.

Edgenora looked pleased. "I simply got tired of showing up at the store and coming home with nothing for meals."

"We were just saying the same thing," said Beatrice wryly.

"It made sense for me to keep something on my phone—something I always have with me. Because, if I don't have any ideas, I end up gravitating to burgers or frozen pizza," said Edgenora.

Wyatt waved the notepad. "Well, we appreciate the help. Otherwise, I fear Beatrice and I would have ended up making ourselves grilled cheese sandwiches for the umpteenth time. And I've been trying to eat healthier lately."

Edgenora, having helped, was now clearly eager to get her grocery shopping done and getting herself back home. "Good seeing you both," she said before striding away, list in hand.

Beatrice and Wyatt peered at the list, brainstorming ingredients they needed and trying to compare them to their somewhat faded memories of what they had at home. They were still creating the list when they heard someone say Wyatt's name.

They turned and saw Quinn Daxton standing there. He had a cart full of mac and cheese boxes and frozen pizzas and looked as if he hadn't slept. Or as if he'd tried to sleep in the clothes he was currently wearing. He had a large mug of coffee in the cart's cupholder.

"Quinn," said Wyatt, looking concerned. "Is everything okay?"

He shook his head. Despite his rumpled appearance, he was still a very handsome man of the tall, dark, and handsome cliché. "I actually planned on calling you later."

Beatrice said, "Should I . . . ?"

Quinn shook his head. "It's okay. It's going to be public knowledge soon, if it's not already. My wife, Tobi, left me yesterday. I'm . . . well, I guess I'm in total shock."

"Of course you are," said Wyatt. "We're so sorry."

Quinn took a deep breath. "It's amazing how fast everything fell apart. The house doesn't even seem civilized anymore. I guess I've found out in just a day's time what a slob I am without having Tobi constantly picking up after me."

Beatrice tried to keep her face neutral and hoped she was doing a good job. She wondered if perhaps Tobi had simply gone on a labor strike.

"Did Tobi give a reason why she was leaving?" asked Wyatt.

Quinn gave a short laugh. "She didn't have to. She found out about the affair I had with Summer shortly before Summer died. I kind of hoped she'd understand that I was planning on ending things with Summer; that I'd realized I wanted to make my marriage with Tobi work. But Tobi just thought the affair ended because Summer had died. Maybe she even thinks I was involved in Summer's death somehow." He gave a hopeless shrug of his shoulders.

Beatrice said, "Were you able to give her an alibi? Were you with Tobi when Summer was found?"

"That's part of the problem. I haven't been sleeping much lately, so I've been getting up really early and just heading downstairs to do some work on the computer. Tobi wouldn't have been able to cover for me, even if she wanted to. And I'm not sure she wanted to. She was really careful not to give Ramsay an alibi for me."

Beatrice said, "How did she find out about the affair?"

Quinn sighed. "She saw a text message from Summer before I could delete it. I guess I'd gotten kind of lazy with covering things up—another sign I needed to end things. This was right before Summer died. I told her I was going to tell Summer that she and I were through. But then Summer was murdered before I had the chance to speak with her. Tobi must have been trying to figure out if she wanted to stick around with me or not, and I guess she made up her mind yesterday."

"You must have a lot of conflicting emotions about Summer's death. It's got to be such a tough ," said Wyatt.

Quinn nodded. "I feel awful about it, of course. On one level, I cared for Summer. But in some ways, her death was . . . not exactly a relief, but closure."

Beatrice, who wasn't very impressed with Quinn's narrative so far, thought it was a rather violent closure.

"Believe me, I'd do anything to take back the fact Summer and I had an affair. I don't know what I was thinking or why I was even tempted. I guess it was the fact that I was flattered by the attention I was getting from Summer. Maybe Tobi and I had gotten too used to each other. Anyway, I really regret it now." He gave Wyatt a twisted smile. "You've got to wonder why I'm telling you all this. Summing up, Tobi left me, and I want her back. Can I schedule some counseling sessions with you?"

Wyatt said, "Of course you can. But is that something Tobi wants to do? Have you spoken with her about it?"

Quinn's shoulders slumped. "I would have talked with her about it, but she won't talk to me. She doesn't take my calls or answer the door when I knock. I thought, maybe, if *you* called and just reached out that it might be better."

Wyatt said quietly, "If Tobi isn't onboard with counseling, I'm not sure it's going to be very productive. But I'd be happy to meet with you one-on-one. I can tell this has got to be hard for you."

Quinn nodded. "That makes sense not to force Tobi into couples counseling. I guess I deserve what's happening, anyway. I was the one who strayed."

Beatrice said, "Maybe you should just give her some time, Quinn. It sounds like she still might be processing everything. She could be more interested in fixing your marriage after a bit of time has gone by."

"Good advice." Quinn sighed. "That's another of my endless faults—impatience. Just another thing I've got to work on, if I have time. The way the cops are looking at me, maybe I'll end up in the clink for the next couple of decades."

"Since you were spending time with Summer," said Beatrice delicately, "were you able to give the police some ideas about who might be a suspect?"

Quinn shrugged. "It's pretty obvious to me that it's Harlowe."

Wyatt said, "Did he know about your relationship with Summer?"

"Did he?" Quinn snorted. "He practically challenged me to a duel. He definitely found out. Besides, he and Summer were having other problems, anyway. She told me they'd been arguing a lot, and that Harlowe was having money problems."

"Money problems? Just on Harlowe's end or for both of them?" asked Beatrice.

"According to Summer, they maintained separate accounts. She said that Harlowe was irresponsible with money. They bought everything separately in case he went into debt—she didn't want the burden of paying off his debts. Her car and the house were in her name, for instance."

Wyatt frowned. "I thought Harlowe was intended to be in charge of the studio's accounts."

"True. Summer said he did a better job keeping the books. He just didn't do a good job with spending less than he made." Quinn shrugged. "I wouldn't have thought she'd have made him the studio manager, but I guess she wanted to give him a shot at it. She was pretty type-A, though. If she'd thought he wasn't doing a good job, she'd have fired him."

Beatrice thought about Dan Whitner and the way Summer had harangued him about his work. She wondered if she'd done the same with Harlowe. Maybe it had been the last straw for him.

She asked, "You said there were people spreading rumors about you and Summer. Do you know who found out about your affair originally?"

Quinn looked grim. "I only wish I did. I'd be sure to give them a piece of my mind." He gave them a tight smile. "I'm sorry I've held you two up for so long. Wyatt, I'll let you know if Tobi agrees to some counseling later on."

With that, he slipped away.

Beatrice realized she'd been holding her breath. She let it go. "He's pretty intense, isn't he?"

Wyatt nodded. "He has a lot to work through."

"He certainly does," said a caustic voice behind them, making them jump. They turned to see Savannah there.

"You scared us to death," said Beatrice with a small laugh. "Gracious."

Savannah gave them a repentant look. "Sorry. I saw Quinn talking with you. He's my neighbor, you know. And I can tell you there's a general lack of order at his house. He's coming and going at all hours. He needs to get himself in order. Since Tobi left, he's been a wreck."

"I didn't realize he was your neighbor," said Wyatt politely.

Savannah snorted. "He was a decent one, but I'm starting to think that's because Tobi was maintaining everything. I live in a tiny house next door, but Quinn and Tobi live in the biggest house in the neighborhood."

"I wonder why Quinn didn't move out if he was the one who was misbehaving," said Beatrice.

Savannah said, "I don't know, but I bet it's because he was hoping they'd work things out and neither of them would have to leave. That apparently didn't go very well."

"I can imagine," said Beatrice.

Savannah said, "I'll leave you two to your shopping. I just came in for a couple of apples." She held up a produce bag.

"You're good not to end up with more than you planned on," said Wyatt wryly. "Whenever I come in the store for one thing, I leave with a cart full."

"You wouldn't do that if you were putting your purchases in a bike basket," said Savannah with satisfaction. "Or if you didn't bring a cart in."

"I'll have to try that," said Wyatt with a smile as Savannah strode away.

Then Beatrice and Wyatt proceeded to get all the ingredients they needed for a quick, healthy dinner and headed home for another quiet evening together.

The next morning, they woke up to Noo-noo barking frantically.

"What time is it?" asked Wyatt groggily.

Beatrice peered at the clock beside the bed. She croaked, "That healthy meal must have made us sleepy. It's nearly seven o'clock."

Wyatt and Beatrice stumbled out of bed and to the door, which is what Noo-noo was pointed at while still barking. Wyatt looked out the side window. "It's Miss Sissy," he said, concern in his voice.

Chapter Eleven

He opened the door and Miss Sissy stood there glaring at them as if they'd taken their sweet time.

"Is everything okay?" he asked with concern. "Come inside and have some breakfast and coffee with us."

That's when Beatrice realized something must indeed be wrong, because Miss Sissy shook her head vehemently. Strands of iron-gray hair fell out of her messy bun. If Miss Sissy was turning down food, she was decidedly worried about something.

"Something's wrong with Sylvia," she spat out.

Beatrice frowned. "Sylvia Hutchins?" The old woman who lived next door to Summer and Harlowe was the only Sylvia she knew.

Miss Sissy nodded. "Didn't come to get me."

Wyatt said patiently, "So Sylvia was supposed to come by your house and pick you up for something?"

Miss Sissy nodded again, more strands of hair falling out of the bun. "The church pancake breakfast."

Now Wyatt looked startled. "The church is having a pancake breakfast?" Wyatt tried to make it to every event the church put on and was panicking now that one had somehow slipped him by.

The old woman said impatiently, "At *her* church."

"Got it," said Wyatt, looking relieved. "Sorry, Beatrice and I have just woken up and might be a little slow."

Miss Sissy didn't look apologetic in the slightest at waking them up. In fact, she looked quite irritated at the slowness Wyatt mentioned. "Needs help!"

Beatrice, like Wyatt, was still trying to put together the threads of what the old woman was saying. "Okay. So we need to go find out what happened to Sylvia. She's not answering her phone?"

More impatient head-shaking.

Beatrice said to Wyatt, "We did oversleep a little. Why don't you get ready to go to work and I'll get dressed and head to Sylvia's with Miss Sissy?"

Wyatt seemed resistant to this idea. "Something could have happened. I'd like to be with you."

"It could just be a misunderstanding," said Beatrice in a low voice.

But Miss Sissy, who had excellent hearing, glared at them. "Something's wrong!" she hissed.

Wyatt wouldn't be dissuaded, however. Which is how, just minutes after they'd gotten up, Wyatt and Beatrice were dressed and driving Miss Sissy to Sylvia Hutchins' house.

They knocked at Sylvia's door and Beatrice rang the doorbell a couple of times. Miss Sissy looked even more agitated than she had before.

"Could she have overslept?" asked Beatrice.

Miss Sissy shook her head vehemently. "Doesn't oversleep!" she spat.

Wyatt tried the door handle. The door opened with a creak. The inside of the house was dim with the rising sun just starting to illuminate spots on the floor.

"Evilllllll," hissed Miss Sissy.

This didn't help with the overall creepy atmosphere. Beatrice shivered.

Wyatt called out, "Sylvia? It's Wyatt Thompson with Beatrice and Miss Sissy."

There was no answer.

Miss Sissy rushed in, looking frantically around her. Then she let out a cry.

Sylvia Hutchins was sprawled on the floor at the bottom of her spiral staircase.

Chapter Twelve

Unfortunately, Sylvia did not have a pulse when Wyatt checked it. Although it looked as if her death could have been an accident, Beatrice phoned Ramsay. Sylvia had lived next door to Summer—what if she'd seen or heard something that Summer's killer wanted to stay secret?

Ramsay came right away, the state police in tow. He greeted them grimly outside the house, where they'd waited for him.

The police officers went inside to confirm Sylvia's death and to tape off the scene. A few minutes later, Ramsay came back outside.

"It does look like foul play," he said soberly.

Miss Sissy made a hissing noise.

Ramsay said to her, "I'm sorry, Miss Sissy. If it makes you feel better, I'm sure your friend never knew what was happening to her."

"Vase was missing," muttered the old woman.

"What's that?" Ramsay cupped his ear.

"Vase was missing!" bellowed Miss Sissy.

Ramsay's gaze sharpened. "Got it. Could you describe the vase?"

Miss Sissy glared at him. "Pink. Hand painted. Pretty. Gone."

Miss Sissy wasn't one to waste words. Ramsay made a note in his small notebook. "Okay. So could you all fill me in?"

So Beatrice and Wyatt told him how Miss Sissy had come over to their house, worried that her friend hadn't picked her up for the pancake breakfast.

Ramsay grunted. "Didn't realize the church was having one today."

"It's at another church," said Wyatt.

"Sylvia was still driving," said Miss Sissy. "Didn't show up."

Ramsay nodded. "Now, Miss Sissy, we want to do everything we can to try and find out what happened to your friend. Do you know of any reason why someone would have wanted to do this?"

Miss Sissy pointed to Summer's house next door, an angry look on her face.

"Right," said Ramsay gently. "Do you know what Sylvia saw? Or what she heard? Did it have something to do with Summer's death?"

But the old woman just glared at him and shrugged.

A voice came from behind them. "Hello? Is everything okay?"

Once again, Harlowe was there at the scene of a crime. But then, supposed Beatrice, Summer's husband did live right next door.

Ramsay said, "Unfortunately, not. Your neighbor has passed away."

Harlowe frowned. "Sylvia? What happened? Did she have a heart attack or something?"

"She met with foul play," said Ramsay somberly.

Harlowe paled. "No. You're sure of that?" Then he quickly added, "Sorry. Sorry. Of course, you are. I just can't believe it.

Who would have wanted to harm her? She wasn't any sort of danger to anyone."

Beatrice had the feeling that someone definitely disagreed with that statement.

"How well did you know Sylvia?" asked Ramsay.

"Not as well as I should have. I could have been a better neighbor, but it always seemed like life was so busy. I spoke with her a few times when we were both out getting our mail or putting our trash out. I always did feel somewhat sorry for her. Sylvia seemed to spend so much time looking out her window at the world instead of engaging in it. I thought she must be lonely."

Miss Sissy shot him an annoyed look. "Wasn't!"

Harlowe looked a bit startled.

Ramsay continued, "Where have you been over the last twelve hours or so?"

"Me?" Harlowe's face grew even paler. "I haven't been anywhere. I was alone in the house. I ate my supper, watched TV, went to bed. Then I heard all the commotion over here and thought I should come over and see what happened. You surely don't think I could have anything to do with this, do you?"

Ramsay didn't answer the question, instead asking him one. "Do you remember the last time you saw Sylvia?"

Harlowe frowned, thinking back. "Actually, yes. I saw her last night before I turned in. I was putting the blinds down and noticed Sylvia looking out her window. I remember thinking that I really needed to make more of an effort to check in with her and make sure she was doing all right."

Miss Sissy made a grumbling sound.

"Do you know what time that was?" Ramsay's voice was intent.

Harlowe said slowly, "It must have been about ten o'clock. I've just been exhausted the last couple of days. I haven't been able to sleep, but I've been turning in early to try to. Then I spend half the night tossing and turning. I can't seem to shut my mind off."

Ramsay said, "Since you've been sleeping poorly, have you noticed any visitors at Sylvia's? Have you seen any cars or heard any noises over here? Kept track of any unusual activity?"

"Evillll," hissed Miss Sissy.

Harlowe gave her a worried look. To Ramsay, he said, "No, I'm afraid not. I must have fallen asleep pretty quickly after I pulled the shades last night. I was awake around three o'clock, but I don't remember hearing anything. Also, I have a white noise machine that I turn on at night. There are neighborhood dogs who bark and they keep me awake." Then he added in an impatient voice, "One thing that would help me sleep better is knowing that whoever murdered my wife was behind bars. I can't believe they're still out walking the streets. Have you made any progress in finding who killed Summer?"

Ramsay raised his eyebrows. "Not considering there's been another death."

"You think the two deaths are connected?" Harlowe's voice rose to a squeak by the end. "I thought maybe it was just a break-in that went wrong."

Ramsay didn't answer, just asked another question. "What type of neighbor was Sylvia?"

"She was perfectly fine as a neighbor. Sylvia kept to herself and wasn't one to play loud music or run the television too loud. She kept her dog inside, so it wasn't one of the ones that kept me up at night."

Ramsay's eyes widened. "She had a dog?"

"Cammie," said Beatrice with alarm, remembering the little dog Sylvia had in her purse at the quilt shop.

Ramsay said, "Y'all didn't notice a dog when you went inside?"

Beatrice and Wyatt shook their heads.

Ramsay frowned. "Is this a big dog we're talking about? Like a lab or something? A dog that might have attacked the intruder?"

Beatrice shook her head again. "Cammie was tiny. She was the kind of dog who fit in Sylvia's purse when she went out."

Ramsay motioned over to a deputy and spoke quietly with him for a few minutes. The deputy nodded and headed into the house.

Ramsay said to Harlowe, "Sorry, you were talking about Sylvia as a neighbor."

"She spent most of her time inside, so she was very quiet. Her yard was kept up by a yardman."

Miss Sissy made a snarling sound, startling Harlowe once again.

Ramsay gave the old woman a calming look. He said, "The thing is, Harlowe, Sylvia spent a lot of time looking out her window, as you mentioned yourself. She may have seen what happened to Summer. You said you hadn't seen anyone over here last night, but have you seen anyone here in general lately?"

Harlowe shook his head. "No one came over here."

Miss Sissy gave a ferocious growl again and Harlowe put his hands up as if in surrender. "Sylvia would sometimes drive away and perhaps she visited with people then." He sounded doubtful, as if he had a tough time picturing Sylvia out cavorting with many friends. "I haven't noticed anyone at the house, though."

"Would you have looked?" asked Ramsay.

"Probably not," admitted Harlowe. "Especially now that I've been so distracted thinking about Summer and trying to figure out my next steps. Although I'd like to think I'd notice if anything seemed unusual over at Sylvia's house."

Ramsay nodded. "I did want to ask you some follow-up questions. Would you like to step away so I can ask them in private?"

Harlowe looked surprised and then glanced at Beatrice, Wyatt, and Miss Sissy. He shrugged. "You can ask me questions right here. I don't have anything to hide."

Miss Sissy scoffed at this and Harlowe reddened a little.

Ramsay said, "I wanted to hear a little more about your financial situation. Yours and Summer's. I understand you kept separate accounts?"

Harlowe nodded. "That's right. Summer liked to do things a particular way. And I guess you could say that Summer was more successful than I was. I've never been particularly ambitious, I suppose. I'm more of the *work to live*, not *live to work* mentality. I also like to think I don't need very much—I'm comfortable with my life and with more simple living. Summer was a bit different in that respect; she wanted more out of life."

"And your marriage? Despite the big differences between you, it worked well?"

Harlowe took a deep breath. "Sorry, it's still a little hard for me to talk about Summer. Yes, we were very different from each other, but most of the time I think that was a positive. Opposites attract, right?"

Beatrice noticed that Ramsay seemed to be considering this. Then he nodded. After all, he and Meadow were very opposite from one another. Ramsay said, "But sometimes, being around someone who's very different can create friction. Did you have any recent arguments or trouble? It seems like life would be pretty stressful with Summer. After all, she was starting a new business, there was construction going on behind your house, and you were in the middle of a job change."

"Actually, it was a very exciting time," said Harlowe, looking rather sad. "Summer said it was enervating, and I fed off her energy. I was very proud of Summer for all she'd accomplished and for having all that drive that I just didn't have. We felt like we were starting a new chapter in our lives and we were looking forward to it. Summer would talk about how convenient it was going to be to step out into the backyard to go to work instead of going on that long commute to Lenoir." He surreptitiously wiped away some moisture in his eyes that was threatening to course down his face.

Ramsay looked curious. "What exactly were you doing to help out with Summer's business? Were you involved in monitoring the construction of the studio and that sort of thing?"

"No, not really. I did keep track of what phase the construction was in and the budget. But Summer liked to keep a handle on the specifics of the construction all by herself. Like I mentioned before, I was more of the office manager."

Since Ramsay still looked curious, Harlowe elaborated. "I came up with the promo campaign for the opening, for instance."

Beatrice found that interesting. After all, the studio had been deserted when Piper and she had arrived on opening day. Either Harlowe hadn't aired the campaign he'd created, or it wasn't very effective at bringing people in.

"But thinking about the construction," continued Harlowe, "have you followed up with Dan, yet?"

Ramsay rubbed his forehead. "See, the thing is, we don't really think Dan Whitner had anything to do with Summer's death."

Harlowe frowned. "He had a pretty good motive, didn't he? Summer was very critical about his work on the studio. Summer talked about the problems with Dan on her social media, even. And she had a good-sized social media following." The last was said with some evidence of pride.

Ramsay made a careful note on his notepad, but didn't comment any further on Dan. "Is there anyone else you can think of who you think Summer might have been at odds with?"

Harlowe slowly said, "Danica has been something of a problem. She's been trolling Summer online."

"Trolling her?" Ramsay's face furrowed.

"Just sort of being mean online," explained Harlowe. "She was using another name and trying to be anonymous, but it was really obvious who she was."

Ramsay said, "And, I take it that's because Summer got Danica fired from the fitness center in Lenoir."

"According to Danica," said Harlowe in a harsh tone. "But according to Summer, that wasn't what happened. The management in Lenoir had gotten complaints about Danica from customers who'd taken her fitness classes."

"Since you knew Summer well, who do you believe?" asked Ramsay.

Harlowe flushed and thought this over for a moment. Then he slowly said, "Usually I'd side with Summer, of course. But I know Danica, and I had a hard time believing that she'd show up late for work or be abrupt with the people taking her classes."

"You'd agree Danica was angry with Summer, though, right? Probably justifiably."

Harlowe nodded. "She was mad. She called Summer from time to time and gave her a piece of her mind. Danica definitely thought that she'd been fired because of something Summer had said or done."

Ramsay said, "You see, Danica says that Summer stole her ideas from her and presented them to the management as her own."

Harlowe looked flustered. "I don't know anything about that. Summer didn't mention anything about it to me."

"Does that sound like something Summer might have done?"

Harlowe paused. Then he looked away from them. "It's possible. Summer was incredibly ambitious. It's probably good that she turned that ambition into her own business. She could be very competitive."

"Having Danica attacking Summer online must have been upsetting for Summer," said Ramsay.

Harlowe looked surprised at the word *upsetting*. "Not really. Summer gave as good as she got. She figured that Danica had other issues with her besides the argument that they had that led to Danica being fired. She believed Danica was jealous of her because Summer was successful and ambitious and always having big ideas about fitness. She built up this huge online following and was going to offer remote personal training sessions in addition to the in-person ones she was already doing."

Ramsay tapped his pencil against his notepad. "Did Danica ask Summer for a job? It seems like she would have, seeing as how Summer was opening up this new place. And because Danica had been out of work for a while."

"Not as far as I'm aware, no."

Ramsay glanced around the group and said, "Again, Harlowe, we can talk in private."

Harlowe bristled. "And again, I don't have any reason to. I don't have anything to hide."

"Yes, but some things are personal and you might not want them aired in public," said Ramsay.

Harlowe stared stubbornly at him. "Go ahead."

Ramsay gave a short sigh. Then he said, "Okay. I understand Summer might have been seeing someone."

Harlowe's face fell into sorrowful folds. "It hurts me to think of it. But I guess I share some of the blame. Summer was always saying I was remote, and she was always trying to engage me. Like I was saying, opposites do attract. Where Summer was always thinking about the next thing and being ambitious, I was quieter. Anyway, sometimes being opposite might push someone into someone else's arms."

"Do you hold any bad feelings toward Quinn?" asked Ramsay quietly.

"Of course I do. I'm only human." He glanced longingly toward his house, as if sorry he ever left it to begin with. "And now, if you're done asking questions, I'm ready to head back home."

Ramsay nodded. "Okay, Harlowe."

As Harlowe walked away, Ramsay said in a tired voice, "Okay. Why don't y'all take Miss Sissy back home, too? She's had quite a day and it's still early. I know where to find her if I need to speak with her again."

Miss Sissy looked mulish, and Ramsay looked to Wyatt and Beatrice for help.

Wyatt said gently, "There's nothing more we can do here, Miss Sissy. You were a good friend to Sylvia. Maybe you can start brainstorming some ways to remember her at her memorial service? As far as I was aware, she didn't have any family."

Miss Sissy hesitated, looking toward Sylvia's door, her lip trembling just a little.

Ramsay said quietly, "I'm sorry about Sylvia. We're going to find out who did this, I can promise you that."

Somewhat satisfied, Miss Sissy turned and headed toward Wyatt's car.

Chapter Thirteen

Beatrice said, "How about if we go back to our house, Miss Sissy? We have all sorts of breakfast things from going to the store last night."

This time, the mention of food had the desired effect. With alacrity, the old woman slipped into the backseat and put her seatbelt on.

Wyatt gave Beatrice a rueful look and murmured, "It looks like a day of distractions might be in order. I wish I could stick around the house and give you a hand."

"Oh, it'll be fine. After we eat, I'll call Meadow. She's watching the baby today and I'll ask her to bring him over."

"Great idea," said Wyatt as they got into the car.

When they got back to the house, Noo-noo grinned at them in welcome from the front window. Miss Sissy and Beatrice headed inside and Wyatt drove away for the church.

The little corgi greeted Miss Sissy excitedly, and she stooped to rub Noo-noo as Beatrice set to preparing a good-sized Southern breakfast of eggs, sausage, and buttery grits.

When it was done, Beatrice set it out on the table. "It won't be Meadow quality," she said, "But I hope it will be good enough." She had the feeling Miss Sissy must be starving. After all, she'd been up early to go to the ill-fated pancake breakfast.

The old woman seemed to think the breakfast was just fine. She plowed through the offerings on her plate rapidly, keeping Beatrice busy refilling it. Beatrice always wondered where the calories went. They never seemed to settle on Miss Sissy's wiry frame.

To keep the old woman's mind off the events of the morning, Beatrice chatted in a rather aimless manner, talking about the weeds she was slaying in her front yard, Boris-the-dog's issues with inappropriate eating, and various adorable things her grandson had said. Miss Sissy seemed very bored with the conversation until Will's name was mentioned.

Her eyes lit up, and she said, "Want to see him."

"Well, you're in luck. I was planning on calling Meadow up and asking her to bring Will by just as soon as we're finished eating."

But Miss Sissy didn't seem to want to wait and set her chin stubbornly. Beatrice bit back a sigh as she pulled her phone out. Will could be a good deal more mature than Miss Sissy was. She was interrupted in her dialing by a rapid knock on the door. Noo-noo exploded into barking.

Miss Sissy's eyes widened. She grabbed a nearby heavy candlestick and held it in a threatening posture as Beatrice cautiously looked out the window.

"It's Meadow and Will," said Beatrice with relief. She wasn't sure who on earth she thought might be at the door, but Miss Sissy had apparently made her quite paranoid.

Miss Sissy put down the candlestick and clapped her hands gleefully. Beatrice opened the door to see Meadow standing there with her hands on her hips, looking cross. Will bounced inside and gave Miss Sissy a big hug. Then the little boy led the old woman by the hand over to the closet, where Beatrice kept the toys for his visits. They proceeded to pull out the entire contents of the closet.

"What is going on?" asked Meadow. "Ramsay won't answer my phone calls and he left this morning before even finishing his bacon. That never happens. Do you know what's happened?"

Beatrice nodded, but looked over at Miss Sissy with concern. "It might be better if we talked privately away from certain folks. I don't want anyone getting upset again."

The only problem was that there was really no space in Beatrice's tiny cottage. Meadow grimaced. "Do we trust Miss Sissy to babysit Will for a few minutes so we can sit in your backyard?" Her expression said that she didn't particularly trust the old woman with such precious treasure.

Beatrice said wryly, "From what I've seen, I'd trust Miss Sissy to guard him with her life."

Beatrice told the old woman that she and Meadow were going to sit out in the backyard for a few minutes. Miss Sissy impatiently waved them away.

As soon as they were seated at the backyard table, Beatrice filled Meadow in as Meadow's face became increasingly indignant.

"You're saying that someone killed *Sylvia Hutchins*? Who on earth would do such a thing? What is the world coming to? Killing innocent little old ladies for sport?" Meadow looked positively apoplectic.

Beatrice said, "I'm not positive Sylvia *was* an innocent old lady. Even if she wasn't, though, she definitely didn't deserve to die because of it. I did have the feeling when we saw her right after Summer died that she was holding something back. I wonder if she saw something the morning of the murder and didn't say anything."

Meadow threw up her hands. "I don't for the life of me understand why people keep important information to themselves. Don't they know that people with secrets always end up dying around here? They should just spill everything they know to Ramsay and avoid the problem completely."

"That's the only thing I can think of that would make someone come after her like that. That she wanted to blackmail the person she saw. We really don't know very much about Sylvia, do we?" Beatrice looked nervously behind her as if Miss Sissy might suddenly be standing there. "Don't say anything to Miss Sissy about any suspicions regarding Sylvia. She'll bite your head off. She apparently thinks Sylvia was practically perfect."

Meadow looked teary suddenly. "Poor Miss Sissy. There she was, at home, waiting for her ride to the pancake breakfast. The ride never came. Then she finds her friend dead. What a terrible morning." She paused. "You know I don't ordinarily give up my time with Will. But, in the interest of distracting and possibly comforting Miss Sissy, I'll let him hang out here for the day while Piper works."

For Meadow, it was equivalent to the ultimate sacrifice. "That's very kind of you, Meadow."

Meadow set her chin bravely. "It's something I need to do." Then her eyebrows furrowed. "We need to stop this madness, Beatrice. Two people dead and Dan Whitner suspected of murder? It's all completely beyond comprehension."

"I'm sure Ramsay will find out who's behind this in no time. He's an excellent police officer."

Meadow made a face. "I'm not so sure. I'm not saying Ramsay isn't perfectly wonderful at his job. But where he truly *excels* is in helping with trespassers, breaking up disputes at the Jaunty Tavern, and handing out speeding tickets. I feel much better when you're around to observe all the little details. Nothing seems to get past you."

"If only that were true," said Beatrice wryly. "I'm sure the perpetrator for these crimes is staring us right in the face and we're just not seeing it."

Meadow gave a violent shiver. "I don't like to think of the murderer as one of our own. It gives me the heebie-jeebies." She sighed. "I guess I'll go run my errands now. I was going to wait and do them all tomorrow, but if I don't have Will today, there are no excuses."

They walked back inside and Meadow gave Will a big hug while Miss Sissy glared at her for interrupting their block building. "You're going to play with your Grandmama and Miss Sissy for a while, okay? See you later, sweetie."

Will beamed up at her and then continued placing farm animals on the tops of blocks as Miss Sissy drove cars around the brightly colored structures they'd constructed.

An hour or so later, Beatrice counted herself lucky that both Will and Miss Sissy got drowsy at the same time. Neither of them seemed able to keep their eyes open.

Beatrice said, "Miss Sissy, would you give me a hand getting Will ready for a morning nap? And you've had a tough day—would you like to put your feet up for a while, too? There's a twin bed in there with the portable crib."

The old woman seemed to like that idea very much. Which is how, twenty minutes later, the sound of snoring emanated from the guest room. Beatrice crossed her fingers that it wouldn't keep Will from falling asleep.

Enjoying the sudden quiet, Beatrice climbed on the sofa and picked up her book. Noo-noo curled up at her feet. Beatrice got so caught up with *Raney* that she didn't notice the time. When Wyatt walked in the door for lunch, she was startled and frowned at the clock. "Gracious, but they've slept a long time."

"Hmm?" asked Wyatt in bemusement. He gave her a quick kiss on the cheek.

"Oh, Miss Sissy and Will are here taking naps," said Beatrice.

Wyatt's bemusement deepened. Then he had a flash of understanding. "I see. So Miss Sissy never did go home after our discovery of Sylvia. And once Will came over, they played so much that they wore each other out."

"That's it in a nutshell."

Beatrice and Wyatt had settled at the table with a couple of tomato sandwiches and some grapes. Wyatt said, "Was Miss Sissy any better?"

"She calmed down once we had a bit of food. Actually, she had a *lot* of food, so I knew she must be perkier than she had been. And then, of course, when Will came over, she was much better. Thank goodness Meadow brought him by. Miss Sissy wasn't in the mood to take no for an answer."

Wyatt said softly, "And how are *you* doing? Two unexpected deaths in one week."

Beatrice took a deep breath. "I'm okay. I think, like Meadow, I'm more focused on wanting to find out who is responsible for all this."

Wyatt was quiet for a few moments. Then he said, "I just want to make sure nothing happens to you."

She reached out, sliding her arm around his shoulders, and he gave her a warm hug. "I'm going to be careful, I promise. People tend to tell me things, as if I were an extension of you, I guess. I'll go right ahead and let Ramsay know. I won't be like Sylvia, who keeps dangerous information to herself."

Wyatt nodded. "That must have been what happened. As Harlowe said, Sylvia spent a lot of time quietly looking out of windows. Why do you think she kept whatever information she had to herself?"

"Well, the more-charitable explanation is that she wasn't exactly sure what she'd seen. Maybe she didn't realize at first that she had important information. Perhaps she even contacted the person involved to see if there was a reasonable explanation." Beatrice considered the question some more. "Sylvia might just have liked knowing things. Maybe the problem was that the murderer saw her at the window and knew she needed to be silenced before she had the opportunity to tell anyone."

Wyatt asked, "And the less-charitable explanation?"

"Is that Sylvia intended on blackmailing the person somehow." Beatrice shrugged. "Somehow I can't quite see that being the case. Sylvia just didn't seem to fit the bill. She was into quilting and her little dog." She suddenly put her hand over her mouth. "Oh my gosh. Poor Cammie. I wonder if the police found her."

"She probably hid if she was really small. I'm sure she's just fine."

Beatrice wasn't so sure. "Maybe she ran out after whoever the killer is. She isn't exactly the kind of dog who can take care of herself."

Wyatt said, "Would you like me to ask Ramsay what happened to Cammie?"

"But he's in the middle of a murder investigation. He probably won't appreciate being pulled away about something like that."

Wyatt said, "I've seen the way Ramsay and Boris interact together. Even though Boris doesn't have the most wonderful manners, Ramsay clearly is devoted to the dog."

"That's true. Would you mind?"

Wyatt pulled out his phone and texted Ramsay. A few moments later, he got a reply.

"Cammie is actually at the police station right now. They're going to look for a potential foster until she can find a permanent home," Wyatt said.

Beatrice said, "Oh, thank goodness she's all right. I'd have been thinking about her all night." She paused. "Do you think you and I could hold on to Cammie for a little while, then? I hate to think of her alone at the police station. She's had such a stressful day."

"It's completely fine with me if that's something you'd like to do. Do you think Noo-noo would be okay with it?"

Noo-noo, who'd been napping near the door to the guest room, perked up as her name was mentioned.

"Well, she gets along with other dogs, even Boris with his terrible manners. I think she might be a little jealous, but mostly okay."

Wyatt said, "Let's give it a go, then. Would you like me to pick her up since you're on Will duty?"

"Could you? Do you have enough time before you need to get back to the church?"

Wyatt said, "I don't have any meetings for thirty minutes, which should be just about the amount of time it will take. I'm imagining there might be some paperwork involved."

And that was indeed the amount of time it took. Wyatt returned and left again, just in time to make his meeting.

Cammie looked exhausted and seemed to droop all over. The haughty look she'd sported when she was in Sylvia's handbag was replaced with an anxious, sad expression. Plus, the poor little dog was shaking.

Noo-noo trotted over to observe Cammie from a distance. Seeing no obvious sign of rejection, the corgi gently sniffed Cammie. Cammie gave her a baleful look, but said hello to Noo-noo, too.

Beatrice gently picked her up, wrapped her in a soft quilt, and held her in her lap for a few minutes, gently stroking her. Gradually, the shaking stopped and Cammie regarded Beatrice with her intelligent, golden-brown eyes.

"It's okay," said Beatrice softly.

And Cammie, taking her at her word, fell right into an exhausted sleep.

When Beatrice heard stirring in the guest room, indicating that Miss Sissy and Will were finally starting to wake up from their long naps, Beatrice carefully put Cammie in an old playpen they used for Will.

Miss Sissy and Will looked a bit surprised to see Cammie. Will said, "Cat!"

"It's actually not a cat but a very little dog," said Beatrice to her grandson. "Would you like to see her? Her name is Cammie."

Will nodded solemnly and gave the dog a curious look. She gave him one in return, never having met a human quite as small as Will was.

"Silvia's dog," said Miss Sissy, peering at Cammie.

Will trotted off to play with his toy cars, giving Beatrice the opportunity to explain.

"The police found her, I'm guessing. I don't have much information about it. Cammie was down at the police station and I felt bad that she was by herself when Sylvia had always given her so much love and attention."

Miss Sissy's eyes grew misty as she looked at the dog. "Love."

"She did really love her. I was startled when she pulled Cammie out of her purse at the quilt shop. Cammie looked at us all as if she thought she was the queen of England."

Miss Sissy chuckled and relaxed a little bit.

Beatrice continued, "Wyatt said that Ramsay mentioned the police were looking for a foster home for Cammie until they found her a permanent place to live."

"Here?" Miss Sissy frowned.

"No, I don't think so. I'm not sure Noo-noo would care for a more permanent arrangement. But we'll keep Cammie for a while until we can find her a suitable home—one Sylvia would think was worthy of Cammie."

Miss Sissy looked satisfied. She gave Cammie a gentle rub and then headed off to play cars with Will.

Beatrice watched the two of them together. She still, for the life of her, didn't know how Miss Sissy was so easily able to get on and off the floor.

The rest of the afternoon was spent quietly. Beatrice cleaned the kitchen while Miss Sissy and Will played until Piper came by to pick Will up. At first, Beatrice wasn't sure if the old woman was going to surrender Will that easily, but she apparently started thinking about her supper. She ended up scampering out the door to pull something together after giving Will a big hug.

Chapter Fourteen

The next morning, right after Wyatt had left for work, Meadow showed up at the door with Boris in tow.

"Good morning!" sang out Meadow as she wrestled Boris inside. "Just thought I'd try to speak with *somebody* about the case. Talking to Ramsay right now is like talking to a brick wall. I should just save my breath."

Noo-noo gave an audible sigh as Boris, clearly in a very keyed-up mood, danced around the kitchen, clearly hoping treats of some kind might be in order. Then the big dog stopped short, staring in gape-mouthed wonder at Cammie.

The tiny dog gave him a stern look.

Meadow's eyes were huge. "Cammie! I'd forgotten all about her."

Cammie looked coldly at Meadow as if she'd expected as much.

Boris cautiously crept forward, wanting very much to say hello to the dog.

"Gracious. She's so little that I'm worried about Boris being around her. He's used to more robust play, you know."

Beatrice did know. Boris's idea of robust play often knocked things off of shelves and tabletops.

Beatrice said, "Why don't you get a firm grip on his leash and let Boris meet Cammie?"

Cammie now shot *Beatrice* a cold look.

"Okay," said Meadow. "Now Boris, you be good. Poor Cammie has had a horrible time of it."

Boris inched forward, sticking his large nose out and then quickly retracting it in a turtle-like way as Cammie, sitting very still, watched.

Finally, Boris gave Cammie a tentative lick on the top of her head. Then he flopped down next to her and rolled over on his back.

Beatrice and Meadow stared at each other.

"He *loves* her," said Meadow. "Look how good he's being."

Boris was indeed being good in a way Beatrice had only seen when he had a stuffed Kong toy. Cammie watched Boris imperiously before curling up next to him.

"Do you think she likes him?" asked Meadow, eyes wide.

It did indeed look that way. Cammie and Boris were soon snoring—Boris in a roof-rattling way and Cammie with gentle little puffs of air.

"She has a very calming effect on Boris," said Meadow, the wheels turning in her mind. "I may have to talk with Ramsay about this."

Beatrice couldn't picture Ramsay wanting to devote much time to the calming effect of Cammie in the middle of a murder investigation.

Meadow said, "If Ramsay sees how quiet and peaceful Boris is around Cammie, he might want *us* to be her new owners. That is, if you're not planning on keeping her?" Meadow gave her a worried look.

"Oh, there's no chance of that. Noo-noo tolerates Cammie just fine, but she likes being the center of our attention too much to want Cammie to be more than a temporary visitor."

Noo-noo was watching Cammie and Boris with interest. Her expression seemed to indicate that she hoped it was the beginning of a beautiful friendship.

Meadow nodded. "Okay. How about if I give Ramsay a little time to warm up to the idea? Since he's right in the middle of a case, it's probably not the right time to ask. In the meantime, I'll come over for short visits to let Cammie and Boris get used to each other."

It looked as if the two dogs had already gotten used to each other, however. Boris had gently wrapped himself around Cammie's small frame as they napped.

Meadow took pictures. Beatrice believed they might be the first non-grandson pictures Meadow had taken for quite a while.

A couple of fairly quiet days went by. Meadow did indeed bring Boris by for visits and Cammie, small as she was, managed to keep the big dog in check with an occasional disdainful look. Beatrice's days were filled with gardening and quilting while Wyatt's were engaged with various church activities and preparation for Summer's memorial service, which he was helping Harlowe plan.

The morning of the memorial service was a stormy one. Beatrice looked out the window with a grimace as the rain poured from the heavens without any sign of letting up.

"It's a good thing Harlowe wanted an indoor service. This storm is pretty intense," said Beatrice.

"I guess we'll be driving over to the church today, even if it is practically next-door to us."

"Oh, definitely. I don't have anything that would protect me from that amount of rain. Just a wimpy windbreaker with a so-so hood. We'll have to drive—and run."

And drive and run they did. In the quick dash from the car to the church under umbrellas, they somehow still ended up getting fairly damp. Fortunately, they'd arrived very early and had plenty of time to dry out before the service started.

"What did Harlowe want for the service?" asked Beatrice.

"He asked for a simple memorial service and for it to take place in the chapel instead of the sanctuary. I had the feeling that he wanted something short so that he could make it through it easier. He said he was having a tough time adjusting."

Beatrice said, "That's probably a lot plainer than what Summer would have planned. It's good that Harlowe picked something that worked better for him."

An hour later, the service started. Piper slipped into the pew next to Beatrice. The service was only lightly attended by a few people in town. Wyatt read a selection from the Bible and gave a short message. Harlowe gave a short eulogy where he spoke briefly about Summer as a lone tear ran down his cheek.

Afterward, they adjourned to the church hall where a few ladies had brought in covered dishes. Beatrice and Piper got some food and sat down at a table. Soon they were joined by Danica.

"Is it all right if I sit here?" she asked them.

"Of course you can," said Piper. "There's plenty of room."

Danica sat down, looking uneasy. "I feel so conspicuous here," she said with a short laugh. "Summer and I weren't exactly friends at the end, you know. But I felt it would look worse if I *weren't* here. Then people really would talk."

Piper said, "It's a good thing you did make it. There aren't so many people in attendance."

Danica said with a sigh, "And I was friends with Summer, at least at the start. I know I pointed out all the problems I'd had with Summer—the work-related stuff. But there were good parts, too. She could make me laugh more than anyone else. We'd crack up sometimes at work, in between classes. Summer was really clever and had these wicked little observations about people."

Beatrice said, "I thought there must have been some good sides to Summer. Piper was a friend of hers, too."

"Not a very close one," said Piper, "but we saw each other every once in a while. I totally agree—she was hilarious. I always smiled around her."

"We saw all kinds of people in the gym, of course. There were people who were exercise junkies and people who were learning how to be personal trainers. There were also folks who had been told by their doctors that they really needed to work out or their health problems would be worse. Summer seemed to see all of them for who they really were."

Beatrice said, "That just goes to show that everyone has a good side."

Danica nodded. "Summer could also stand up for you. One time I had this really awful client who made me totally miserable. He was always trying to make moves on me and never seemed to take a hint. I kept trying to rebuff him, but he never stopped."

"And Summer said something to him?" asked Beatrice.

"Summer told him she was going to fill his wife in as soon as she saw her. He left with his tail between his legs." Danica had a small smile on her face from the memory.

"Did Summer just change into a difficult person overnight, or was there always that side of her personality there?" asked Piper.

Danica shrugged. "She definitely got worse. At first, I thought she must have an unhappy marriage. But then I met Harlowe and realized he was totally amazing. He was just so proud of her and supportive. Exactly what you'd want in a husband."

"So you realized Harlowe wasn't the problem," said Beatrice.

"Exactly. That's when I started wondering if her money and her ambition changed her. Summer started acting as if she was better than anyone else. She stopped caring about people's feelings." Danica rubbed her eyes as if she were exhausted. "So that's Summer. Now we have another death to handle—Sylvia's. And the police have been talking with me about it."

"Did you know her?" asked Piper.

Danica shook her head. "I didn't know her at all. But it makes me feel sick that someone did something like that. And I don't understand why Ramsay thinks the two deaths are related. Sylvia didn't sound like the kind of person who'd have known Summer or been in one of her classes."

Beatrice said, "Sylvia was Summer's next-door neighbor. A particularly observant one."

Danica's eyes widened. "Got it. Someone killed her because she .knew who murdered Summer? That's awful. But why didn't

Sylvia just tell the police? Was she planning on doing something with the information? Blackmailing the killer or something?"

Beatrice shook her head. "I'm not sure." She paused. "Considering you've been looking for a job, I'm guessing you didn't ask Summer if you could work at her new studio? With everything that happened, I suppose you wouldn't have wanted to work for her."

Danica colored. "I didn't, no. It was obvious to me that Summer's studio was going to be all about Summer. She was planning on being the only instructor there."

Piper frowned. "What if she needed to take a sick day or something? She didn't want anyone there for backup?"

"Summer? Sick?" Danica gave a harsh laugh. "Summer had no intention of being sick, ever. And viruses apparently understand that because she never caught anything. She seemed immortal. It's one of the reasons it's hard to wrap my head around the fact that she's gone."

Piper said, "Thinking back on asking for jobs, did you get in touch with the school?"

"I did. I have an interview set up with the administration. I'm a little nervous about it. I don't have any formal experience in education."

Piper said, "But you have lots of experience and knowledge in fitness and teaching fitness classes. Right now, they have no one."

Danica brightened at that. "True."

"Just try to focus on how much you love encouraging people to be their healthiest selves. It's clear you're really passionate about exercise and eating right." Beatrice glanced at Danica's plate. It had raw vegetables, raw fruits, and some salad with no dressing on it.

Danica followed Beatrice's gaze and laughed. "It may look like I'm depriving myself all the time, but that's really not it. I've just gotten so used to eating healthy foods that when I don't, my body sort of flips out. I don't like the stomach upset I get when I eat junk." She hurriedly added, "Not that the church ladies are serving junk food."

Beatrice chuckled. "It's a good thing they didn't hear you say that. But you're right—it's heavy food, for sure. Lots of gravies and fried foods. If you're not used to it, I can imagine your stomach would revolt. Anyway, if you can translate your passion for healthy lifestyles into the interview, you'll be great. That will help keep you from feeling nervous if you think of it as just sharing what you know."

Danica nodded. "That sounds like a smart plan. I've just been jittery lately, regardless, what with the police talking to me and everything. I hope the cops get who's behind all this, and fast." She paused and said in a low voice, "I know I was thinking before that Harlowe must have something to do with this. But he seems so genuinely broken about Summer's death that it's hard to believe he could have been involved. If he is that good of an actor, he should be on the stage. Now I'm feeling bad that I told Ramsay he must have done it."

"I know you said Harlowe is a good guy," said Piper.

"Exactly. I always thought he was a real saint for putting up with Summer. Love is hard to understand, I guess. Anyway, enough about me and all my drama. How are things going with both of you?"

They chatted for a while as they ate. When they were finished, Danica said, "I'd better run. I've got to find something decent to wear for the interview. Good talking with y'all."

As she left, Piper said, "I should be going, too, so I can give Meadow a break from watching the baby."

Beatrice said wryly, "Meadow won't forgive you for picking him up early. You know how she is about her time with him."

"That's true. I wanted to get Will a haircut, though. His wispy hair is a little out of control."

Beatrice laughed. "You'll probably have to take Meadow with you. She'll want to take pictures or video the whole thing."

"Oh my gosh, I didn't even think of that! You're totally right. Well, maybe she'll be a distraction for him. I'm not sure he's all that crazy about getting haircuts." She bent to give Beatrice a peck on the cheek. "See you soon, Mama."

Chapter Fifteen

Beatrice was finishing up her glass of lemonade and was about to get ready to leave, herself, when she spotted Ramsay heading her way. He raised a hand, and she pointed to one of the empty seats next to her.

He joined her, sitting down with a plop. "How are you, Beatrice? Aside from being at a funeral, I mean."

"I think the question is more how are *you* doing, Ramsay? I know it's always tough to find time to even eat or sleep during these investigations."

"It is. Meadow's been fussing at me, of course. At least she's distracted with the baby today. But it's one of those cases where it just doesn't feel like we're getting anywhere. Everything seems to be leading to a dead end." He shrugged and rubbed his eyes tiredly.

Beatrice said, "I d have a question for you. Do you know why Sylvia didn't just tell you what she'd seen? I know I'm just assuming she saw something the morning Summer was murdered, but it does seem the most likely scenario."

Ramsay sighed. "I've been thinking about this. I'd go by and knock on Sylvia's door from time-to-time to do a wellness check on her. I felt bad that she was all alone over there and didn't go out much—despite what Miss Sissy has said. I think their pancake breakfast outing was a regular event, but Sylvia didn't do a whole lot of other stuff. Anyway, I've always gotten the feeling that she was real observant and, also, that she just liked *knowing* stuff. She got a charge out of being the one who was in the know.

So she'd peer out her windows and see what was going on with the neighbors."

"Did she gossip about the things she knew? Did she tell you about them, for instance, when you'd come over for your wellness visits?"

He nodded. "Sometimes. It was always harmless gossip. She was the first to tell me about the construction going on behind Summer's house, for instance. Sylvia looked a little smug when she knew something that no one else did. So maybe she was planning on telling Miss Sissy at their outing what was going on next door. But she never got the chance."

"Why would Sylvia have opened her door to a killer if she knew who they were?"

Ramsay said, "When I followed up with Miss Sissy, she mentioned that Sylvia always left her door unlocked. She'd grown up in Dappled Hills and had always felt safe enough in the community not to worry about locks."

"And you definitely don't think Sylvia was planning on blackmailing the murderer?"

"Nope," said Ramsay. "She had plenty of money. When her husband died, she lived very frugally. She wasn't interested in an extravagant lifestyle. She didn't even spend the money she had, so why would she want more?"

"Not to be nosy, but do you know where the money will go?"

Ramsay grinned at her. "That actually *is* really nosy. But I'm sure it'll be public knowledge soon, if it's not already. She has a distant cousin she's leaving some money to. But she's also settling some cash on Miss Sissy."

Beatrice raised her eyebrows. "Really?"

"She seemed to be Sylvia's main, if not her only, friend. I haven't spoken with Miss Sissy about it, though. I'm doing that shortly."

Beatrice mused, "Miss Sissy with money. I can't imagine what that's going to look like."

Ramsay chuckled. "I have the feeling Miss Sissy will just go on as usual. Nothing really seems to change with her." He snapped his fingers. "I've been meaning to ask you. How did you like *By the Pricking of My Thumbs*?"

"It scared me to death. But that might be because I read it at the same time that I discovered a murder. I stayed up half the night reading it and didn't sleep. It was great, but . . . yeah."

Ramsay smiled at her. "I guess the timing could have been better, couldn't it? What are you reading now?"

"Remi recommended a Clyde Edgerton book. *Raney*. It's a more upbeat novel. But I'm glad you recommended the Agatha Christie. I hadn't really read any of the Tommy and Tuppence books and I'll check some others out soon." She paused. "I'm almost scared to ask what you're reading. It's probably some sort of ominous tome."

"Well, like you, I chose the wrong time for my current read. It's *Finnegans Wake*."

Beatrice said, "For heaven's sake. Is there ever a good time to tackle James Joyce?"

"Probably not. But especially not during a murder investigation. It's a pretty challenging read."

He paused. "How are things going with your little roommate? I hear you took in Cammie."

"As a temporary measure. She's actually a pretty neat dog. Cammie minds her manners very well and seems to realize she's a guest. She doesn't try to steal Noo-noo's food or toys and walks very politely with us when we head out for walks."

"But you're not wanting to keep her full-time."

"No, I think Noo-noo would be happier if Cammie just visited us from time-to-time instead of living with us."

Beatrice wondered if Meadow had brought up the fact that she'd brought Boris over to see Cammie a few times. She'd decided to keep quiet about it just in case she hadn't, but then Ramsay brought it up, himself.

"I hear Cammie has a very calming effect on our wild dog. Meadow said something about Boris visiting her?"

Beatrice nodded. "It's pretty amazing. She just gives him a stern look, and he settles right down. Then they curl up together and fall asleep."

"That's something I'll have to see for myself to believe," said Ramsay with a chuckle. He glanced at his watch. "Okay, well, I better get back to it. Good talking with you, Beatrice."

Beatrice glanced across the room to Wyatt, who was speaking with some members of the congregation. Before she could join him, she heard someone call her name.

"Remi," said Beatrice with a smile.

Beatrice was surprised to see Remi at the funeral. Perhaps, like Danica, she'd thought people in Dappled Hills would talk if she weren't there. Remi said, "Can I sit here with you for a few minutes?"

"Please do," said Beatrice, gesturing to a chair.

Remi put her plate down and sat next to Beatrice. She smiled at her. "How's *Raney* going?"

"I haven't had a chance to read too much, but what I've read is excellent. Great suggestion, Remi." Beatrice paused. "I have to admit I'm a little surprised to see you here, after our last conversation."

Remi gave her a wry smile. "Yeah, I know. But I got to thinking, and I realized that if I didn't come, I really wouldn't have any closure at all. I'm all about closure. I need to close the Summer chapter of my life . . . when we were actually friends . . . and start a new, post-Summer chapter."

"That makes sense. What did you think of the service?"

Remi quickly said, "Well, Wyatt always does a terrific job, of course. And it was perfect in every way. Probably a lot quieter than Summer would have wanted, though."

"In terms of the number of people in attendance?"

"That, and also the lack of a choir and instruments. I have the feeling Summer would have thrown a huge funeral," said Remi wryly.

Beatrice thought about how Danica had spoken about Summer changing. She said, "While you knew Summer, was she always the same? I mean, did she seem to change significantly over the period you knew her?"

Remi shrugged. "I'm not sure if she changed all that much. I'm thinking it's more that *I* changed. At first, I was a lot more tolerant of Summer's mean jokes. She also just sort of *picked* at people. I remember she could really tease you if there was some aspect of your appearance that she didn't like. I didn't let it bother me at first."

"And then you changed?" asked Beatrice.

Remi nodded. "Not soon enough. I should have pushed back at her and told her to stop being ugly to me and other people. I should have stood up for myself. After Summer lied about approaching Quinn for me, I realized how much I'd put up with over the years. Even though she was mean, I still thought of her as a friend. But she totally lost my trust after the whole Quinn thing. I'd trusted Summer, and she'd just served her own purpose."

"Why do you think Summer didn't try to speak with Quinn for you?"

Remi said, "I've thought about that. I think she just didn't want to see me happy. She was that kind of person, no matter what Harlowe thought of her. I guess she wasn't as mean to him as she was to other people."

Beatrice wasn't entirely sure that was the case. "What did you make of Sylvia's death? Did you know her?"

"I just saw her around town every once in a while—in the grocery store or something. But I didn't know her. Am I right that she was Summer's neighbor? Someone told me that. But I've never been to Summer's house, so I wouldn't know."

Beatrice nodded. "Sylvia lived directly next door to Summer."

"So the police are thinking Sylvia saw something the morning Summer died?"

"That's right," said Beatrice.

Remi gave a shiver. "This is all so messed up. I haven't been able to sleep since all this started. I keep getting up at night and making sure I locked my door. I imagine I'm hearing noises at night in my house."

Beatrice noticed Remi did look exhausted. There were dark circles under her eyes.

Remi gave a short laugh. "I didn't even tell you the other thing. I ran into Quinn downtown yesterday and we got to talking. He told me his wife had left him and that his whole life was falling apart. Tobi was gone. And that the only person he'd ever really wanted to date was me. That he'd asked Summer before he started seeing Tobi if I was dating anyone. Summer had lied to him and told him I was seeing someone."

Beatrice sighed. "Oh, no. So Summer totally sabotaged a potential relationship from both ends."

"That's right." She paused and looked uncomfortable. "I hate to say this because on some level, I still have feelings for Quinn. But something Quinn told me just didn't seem to add up."

"About Summer, you mean?"

Remi nodded. "Quinn said he'd mentioned to Summer—the day before she died—that he needed to break off their affair. Apparently, he told her he was going to try and make his relationship with Tobi work. He said he went on about the fact that he didn't really like himself anymore because he thought of himself as a cheater. Quinn said he wanted to change back into being someone he felt proud of."

"Did he say how Summer reacted to him breaking up with her?"

"He said Summer was in a bad mood at the time. That a tree had fallen down in her yard, narrowly missing the studio. Quinn said Summer basically threw him out of there," said Remi. "But I drive by Summer and Harlowe's on the way to the library and that tree wasn't there the day before Summer died. I passed by there on my way home at six p.m."

"You saw the tree down the day after that?"

"Exactly. I saw a bunch of emergency vehicles there, too, that morning. Now I know they were all at Summer's because she'd been murdered, of course. At the time, I thought the tree must have fallen and maybe harmed the property or someone."

Beatrice said slowly, "So you're thinking Quinn might have murdered Summer? Maybe because Summer didn't want to end the affair? That maybe he got frustrated with her during an argument and lashed out?"

Remi gave a short laugh and rubbed her eyes. "I don't know. I'm so exhausted that I don't even know what I'm talking about. Plus, the police attention isn't helping much. If they think I killed Summer over a guy, they're crazy."

"I'm sure they're just following protocol."

Remi said, "I mean, I wasn't *happy* with Summer and I realized my friendship with her wasn't a healthy one. But it certainly didn't turn me into a murderer."

Remi paused and looked at Beatrice. "I'm sorry. I've got you looking really stressed out. This isn't what you signed up for when you came to Summer's funeral."

Beatrice said, "I think I was pretty stressed out before, actually. I'm just hoping the police find out who's responsible for these deaths soon. I'm ready for everything to return to normal again."

"I get that. Me too. It's kind of hard to get away from people talking about it. Even in the library, that's all the patrons have been wanting to talk about. It's just the way it is in Dappled Hills." She glanced at her watch. "Well, I'd better be heading out. Good to see you, Beatrice."

After Remi left, Beatrice joined Wyatt, who was just going up to speak with Harlowe again. They spoke for a few minutes. Harlowe seemed pleased with how the service had gone, but he also looked understandably exhausted. It wasn't long before Wyatt and Beatrice left to head back home.

Fortunately, the sheeting rain had stopped, and a lazy drizzle was falling.

"Quiet afternoon at the house?" asked Wyatt.

"Most definitely. I could use some time to just relax for a while."

Wyatt asked, "You're planning on reading? Or quilting? Or possibly even napping?"

"After all the food I ate at the funeral reception, I probably *will* end up napping," said Beatrice ruefully. "But I'd like to do a little quilting. I had to hurry and finish the UFO for the guild meeting and now I think I'd like to do some leisurely quilt work."

They got back home, let Noo-noo out, and then settled into the living room. Wyatt worked on a Sudoku puzzle, and Beatrice sat at her sewing machine.

But apparently, Beatrice had too much on her mind. She accidentally chose the wrong stitch on the sewing machine. Unfortunately, she didn't notice her mistake until quite a few stitches had been made. "What on earth?" she muttered.

"Something wrong?" asked Wyatt.

"I just made a bunch of stitches that I don't even recognize." Beatrice studied them, shaking her head.

"You chose the wrong setting by accident?"

"Wrong stitch, wrong presser foot. Everything is wrong." Beatrice sighed and looked up what stitch she had actually ended up using. "Looks like I just made a bunch of shell tuck stitches."

"That doesn't sound good," said Wyatt.

"You're right. It's supposed to be used for scalloping. I'm going to have to pluck all of these out." She rubbed her forehead. "And this is supposed to be my relaxing hobby."

"Could you just use the stitch, anyway?"

Beatrice said, "Well, it closed up the gap, but no. My perfectionism wouldn't allow that." She put the quilt aside with a sigh. "Maybe it's best if I just read for a while."

"We could talk," suggested Wyatt.

Beatrice sighed again. "I feel like all I want to talk about is Summer and Sylvia. And that's probably not going to help me relax."

Wyatt said, "How about if we talk about the baby? That always seems to cheer you up."

Beatrice smiled. "It does. Will is doing really well. He actually drew this amazing picture at preschool the other day. Did I tell you about it? It's the first time he didn't draw a line for the sky."

And, with gentle conversation and the assistance of a glass of white wine, Beatrice put the day behind her.

Chapter Sixteen

Another couple of days passed. Sunday, naturally, was church and Beatrice winced as Ace, the cell phone guy, managed another interruption. Piper and family came over for another lunch after church. The afternoon was busy because Wyatt and Beatrice both went to visit hospitalized church members.

When Monday morning came, it seemed as if it would be a quieter day. Wyatt and Beatrice decided on a hot breakfast. Beatrice made some cheese grits and started the coffee while Wyatt whipped up scrambled eggs and some sausage links.

Wyatt said, "You've had a really rough last seven days. How about if you and I go to lunch today?"

"Your schedule is open around lunchtime?" asked Beatrice, a doubtful tone in her voice.

"It is. I'm not quite sure how that happened, but I'm going to take advantage of it. How about the bistro downtown?"

Beatrice said wryly, "That's a bit of a splurge, isn't it?"

"I think we deserve it. How about noon?"

So their date was set. Noo-noo watched with interest as they loaded their plates with breakfast food and sat down at the table.

Once Wyatt had headed off for the church, Beatrice took Noo-noo for a long walk. It was a slow one, but Beatrice enjoyed those almost more. Noo-noo would stop and sniff at various things and each time she did, Beatrice tried to find something interesting, herself. She saw a monarch perched on a butterfly bush one time and a box turtle lumbering off into the woods another. Noo-noo, of course, was more preoccupied with what *couldn't* be seen, but smelled. They ambled around Dappled Hills for about an hour before heading back to the house.

Fortified by her walk, Beatrice decided to attack the messed-up quilt stitching. Putting it off only made things worse, she told herself. Then it might even end up being an unfinished quilt, itself.

Pulling out the shell tuck stitching didn't take as long as Beatrice had feared. Soon she was back at the sewing machine and making forward progress. In fact, time completely slipped away from her. Before she knew it, it was time to get ready for her noon lunch with Wyatt.

She was trying to make sense out of her hair when her phone rang. "Wyatt?" she asked. "Is everything okay?"

Wyatt said ruefully, "I'm afraid things could be better. Ramsay called to say Miss Sissy has set out on foot to find out who killed Sylvia."

"Oh, for heaven's sake," muttered Beatrice. Ramsay knew Wyatt had a very calming effect on Miss Sissy and she wasn't surprised he'd called her.

"I know. Would you mind if we set out a few minutes early and try to dissuade her from having her own investigation?"

Beatrice said, "Well, I'll *mind*, but I totally agree it's the right thing to do. She'll be yelling at people and acting as if she knows more than she does. That's all we need now is a third victim."

"I'll be right there in the car."

Beatrice quickly finished getting ready, grabbed her purse, and stepped outside just as Wyatt was pulling up in the car.

"Ramsay said there were reports of Miss Sissy over near Sylvia's neighborhood," said Wyatt. "Ramsay never actually saw her himself; he just thought she might come if you and I tried persuading her."

Beatrice snorted. "More like if *you* persuaded her. Miss Sissy definitely tends to listen to you more than she does me. If you can distract her, I can probably hustle her into the car before she launches herself at me."

They drove around for a while very slowly, calling out the windows from time to time. Beatrice felt as though they were searching for a particularly recalcitrant cat.

Finally, they spotted her. She was several houses down from Summer's house, banging on the front door while the occupant was looking balefully out the front window.

"There she is," said Wyatt.

"And she does look very riled up." Beatrice sighed.

Miss Sissy was indeed riled up. Her hair had completely fallen out of her messy bun, making her look rather wild. She was pounding on the front door, demanding to be let in.

"Did she just say *in the name of the law*?" asked Wyatt quietly.

"I suppose she's deputized herself."

The old woman turned as they called out to her. Her chin jutted out stubbornly.

"Miss Sissy," said Wyatt gently, "I know you want to help find out what happened to your friend. You must feel very hurt. You've been a very good friend to Sylvia."

Miss Sissy's lip trembled just a bit, but she didn't move.

Wyatt continued, "Unfortunately, I think the police are better-suited to investigating. It could be very dangerous for you if you get involved. We just don't want anything to happen to you. You're very special to us."

Miss Sissy smiled at him a little. It was the first smile Beatrice had seen from the old woman in a long while. Aside from when she was with Will, of course.

But Miss Sissy still seemed stubbornly set on doing a house-to-house inquiry. Wyatt finally added, "Beatrice and I are about to head off for a nice lunch. Would you like to join us?"

Miss Sissy's eyes lit up, and she immediately turned and headed for their car.

Wyatt gave Beatrice a rueful look. "Sorry," he whispered.

She smiled at him. "It's okay."

Fortunately, the establishment at the restaurant didn't seem in the least perturbed by the fact Miss Sissy appeared even more unkempt than usual. They seated them at a table covered by a white tablecloth right in front of the window.

The meal was indeed a splurge. Beatrice winced a little as she glanced at the menu. It all sounded mouth-watering, but pricey. There was a crab linguine, sesame seared salmon, shrimp and grits, and a summer risotto. She'd decided on the risotto since it was basically a vegetable plate with baby heirloom tomatoes, basil pesto, and crudo . . . it was a bit less-expensive.

She was particularly glad of her modest choice when Miss Sissy ordered *several* things off the menu. It was a move that made even Wyatt look a bit anxious.

After the server had walked away, Miss Sissy said gruffly, "I'm paying."

"Miss Sissy, you don't need to do that. It's our treat—we invited you," said Wyatt.

Beatrice was thinking, rather ungraciously, that they should let the old woman pay for it if she could.

Miss Sissy shrugged. "Sylvia is paying for the meal." She looked sad. "Left all her money to me."

Wyatt said kindly, "Which was so thoughtful of her. But the will has to go through probate, of course. It will be a while for that money to show up."

She gave him a determined look, setting her chin. "Still paying. Have my own money."

This came as a surprise to Beatrice. The old woman certainly didn't live as though she had a dime to her name. She was fond of wearing the same clothing every day (they were always clean, at least), and a wilderness of bushes and weeds had grown up around her small home.

Wyatt tried to gently push for paying, but Miss Sissy glared at him and reiterated that she was going to take care of the bill.

That settled, Beatrice tried to steer the subject into very non-Sylvia channels. It was obvious immediately that this tactic was not going to work as Miss Sissy dragged the conversation back to her friend.

"I know who did it," she muttered, fury in her narrowed eyes.

Wyatt looked startled. "You know who was responsible for Sylvia's death?"

Miss Sissy spat out, "That woman."

Beatrice said, "Which woman, Miss Sissy? We need to tell Ramsay if you know who did it."

There were quite a few women who potentially could have murdered Summer and Sylvia. Remi, Danica, Tobi—Miss Sissy needed to narrow the field down.

"It's *obvious*," said Miss Sissy, her voice dripping scorn.

"Unfortunately, it's not obvious to me," said Beatrice. "Did Sylvia tell you something?"

"Didn't get to eat pancakes with Sylvia," snarled Miss Sissy.

"Yes, but didn't you speak with her on the phone before then? To set up your trip to the church breakfast? And maybe just chat?" Despite the question, Beatrice was having a hard time envisioning Miss Sissy having a civilized conversation on the phone with anyone. Speaking with her on the phone was always something of an adventure. She'd bark at you and then never say goodbye—just abruptly hang up. Then you'd be standing there with a dead phone next to your head.

Miss Sissy seemed disinclined to answer so Beatrice pressed, "Did Sylvia see something the morning Summer died?"

"If she did, and she told you," said Wyatt quietly, "then you could be in danger yourself, as we were explaining earlier. It's best to go to Ramsay and tell him everything you know. We can even go with you, if you like."

"Don't know her name," growled Miss Sissy.

"Could you describe her?" asked Beatrice, trying not to sigh in exasperation.

"Didn't see her! Sylvia told me about her. Said she was mad at losing money. Sylvia heard her!"

Beatrice looked at Wyatt. Was it Danica, then? Upset about losing her job and income?

Just then, the food arrived at the table. Miss Sissy decided their conversation was over as she launched into her meal.

After lunch, Wyatt said, "Should I take you back home, Miss Sissy?"

The old woman shook her head. "Want to see Maisie."

The Patchwork Cottage was right down the street, so Miss Sissy trotted off to see the shop cat and Wyatt and Beatrice got into the car.

"Do you want to go back to the house?" asked Wyatt.

Beatrice said, "How about if I go to the church with you? I can check in with Edgenora for a few minutes, and then I'll walk back home." The church was very close to their house, so it wasn't much of a walk, but after the big lunch Beatrice had eaten, she thought every little bit might help. And, besides speaking with Edgenora, there was a sunny little courtyard at the church that Beatrice enjoyed sitting in. It was full of rose bushes and other flowering bushes and was a beautiful spot for reflection or just relaxation.

Wyatt hurried off, running behind, for a meeting of the church elders. Beatrice had a brief chat with Edgenora before the phone rang and Edgenora got pulled into some church business. So Beatrice set off for the courtyard. The sun was dappled through a tree and Beatrice raised her face to the light, enjoying the dose of vitamin D.

There was a tap on the door leading outside, and Beatrice opened her eyes to see Tobi there. She smiled at her and gestured for Tobi to join her.

"Sorry," said Tobi, looking apologetic. "I didn't mean to disturb you. This looks like a wonderful spot here."

"It's my favorite place at the church, aside from the sanctuary. How are you doing? You seem very chipper."

Tobi grinned at her. "I just presented those ideas for the new youth program at the church to the elders. It sounds like they're planning on adopting them."

"What? That's great news, Tobi! You must be very proud. I know it took a lot of work to brainstorm, plan, and then present the program."

She nodded, ruefully. "When you suggested I speak to the youth director about it, I realized I needed to have more than just an idea. I came up with a real proposal, so it seemed a lot more professional. And I'm glad I did. Anyway, I feel like I'm starting a new chapter in some ways."

Beatrice didn't want to bring up her separation from Quinn, so waited to see if she would. And, a moment later, Tobi did.

"I hear Quinn isn't doing so well on his own. That the house quickly became a disaster." Tobi shrugged. "But then, I'd pretty much done all the inside work on the house. I bet it must be a real mess in there."

Beatrice said, "I'm sorry you're going through this. It must be really hard."

Tobi nodded. "At least we're not putting kids through it. That would be even worse. That was something else we weren't getting along about. I'd always wanted kids, and I thought Quinn was on-board with that. But he changed his mind from when we'd first talked about having kids. He decided he liked having the freedom for us to do whatever we wanted to do without being tied down." She gave a short laugh. "But then we never *did* anything. I mean, that's fine if it's your excuse, but at least go on a vacation."

Beatrice said, "Was there something in particular that made him change his mind?"

"You've got me. I think he *never* really wanted kids and was just scared to say anything because he knew that would have ended our relationship right then. He knew I always planned on having a family. Anyway, now that we're spending some time apart, I'm going to take the opportunity to try and get my head straightened out so I can figure out what it is I want."

"Whether you want to be with Quinn or not?" asked Beatrice.

"Right." Tobi sighed. "Part of me wants to sweep in there and clean up all his mess and tell him it will be okay. You know—go save Quinn. But part of me says he can just suffer for a while. I barely even feel as if we're separated because he keeps calling me all the time. That's driving me crazy, actually."

"Asking you to come back to him?" asked Beatrice.

"That's right. And he shows up at the place I'm renting, too, looking pitiful. I mean, he's making *me* feel bad, and he's the one who cheated. I guess it's the only time he's done it, but we haven't even been married very long. It's a bad sign, don't you think?"

The elation that had been on her face coming out of the meeting had faded. Tobi looked questioningly at Beatrice.

Beatrice said slowly, "I'm not sure that's for me to decide, Tobi."

Tobi looked as if she wasn't really listening. "I've been thinking about talking with Wyatt about the whole thing. Not couples counseling—more like using Wyatt as a sort of sounding board."

"That's a good idea. He's a great listener and is good with advice, too."

Tobi gave a short laugh. "That's good. I need all the advice I can get. The police are talking with me about Sylvia's murder now, too."

"Oh, no," said Beatrice.

"I guess I should have realized that was going to happen, considering she lived right next door to Summer. And poor Sylvia always had something of a reputation for being nosy. I wish I'd known in advance that I needed an alibi. Instead, there I was at my rental place, alone. It only serves to make me look guilty."

"Did you know Sylvia?"

Tobi shook her head. "Not at all. I mean, I knew where she lived and that she was nosy just because people talk. I got the impression she didn't get out much. I feel bad about what happened to her." She put her hand over her mouth. "Oh my gosh, I just realized you were the one who found her."

"I was with Wyatt and Miss Sissy," said Beatrice.

"I'm so sorry. I shouldn't even be talking about this to you. It must be really upsetting."

Beatrice said, "It definitely was. But I'm thinking at this point that talking through it seems to help."

Tobi nodded. "I get it. With something like that, maybe it's not a good idea to keep everything bottled inside. Anyway, I do feel bad for Sylvia. She had such a quiet life and then something really violent happened to her at the end. It's awful." She paused.

"I know you spend a good deal of time with Meadow and Ramsay. Do you have any sense over whether Quinn is considered a major suspect or not?"

"Should he be?" asked Beatrice.

Tobi snorted. "Who knows? He was already up and dressed when I got up the day Summer died. Maybe he'd been out of the house and maybe not."

Beatrice kept her face neutral. If Quinn had been out of the house, that means Tobi didn't have an alibi either. He wouldn't have known for sure if she were awake or not.

Beatrice said carefully, "I'm sure the police, as a matter of protocol, are going to speak with anyone they'd previously spoken with about Summer's death."

"It's so frustrating. I wasn't even that mad at Summer. It's not as if Summer and I were close friends or anything; that would have made her affair with Quinn seem more of a betrayal. Instead, I hold Quinn 100 percent responsible. In a way, she did me a favor. I'm much happier on my own. I'm not great financially, but my parents are helping me out until I can find a full-time job. They said they'd pay for tuition if I wanted to go back to school. All of this brainstorming on youth programming made me realize how much I enjoyed that stuff. I could get certified as a teacher."

Beatrice said, "I'm sure Piper would be happy to talk with you about teaching, if you needed someone to bounce the idea off of."

Tobi brightened. "Thanks. That's a great idea."

"I hope things work out for you. I know you're having a rough time."

Tobi said, "I just hope the cops realize Summer wasn't worth going to jail over. And I didn't even know Sylvia. I'm ready to move forward with my life. I'm definitely going to talk to Wyatt about my marriage, but mostly because I want to put it behind me. I need to get my life back on track. Maybe down the road I'll find someone else, but I don't feel like I *have* to find someone. That's a major change because I've always felt like I needed to be part of a couple." She smiled at Beatrice. "Sorry, I've talked your ear off."

"Not a bit. I'm just glad to hear everything is starting to look up for you."

Tobi and Beatrice walked toward the church exit together, talking about lighter subjects. Then Tobi drove off as Beatrice walked back to the house.

She'd been gone for a while, so decided to take Noo-noo for a walk to stretch her legs. The little dog yawned and rolled over on her back when Beatrice got the harness, making Beatrice laugh. "You're being lazy today! You always love going on walks."

Noo-noo gave her an upside-down grin from the floor.

So instead, Beatrice curled up on the sofa with her book for a while. She read several chapters of *Raney* and then took a delicious nap afterward. Noo-noo decided to do the same.

Beatrice woke with a start and a gasp about an hour later. She'd startled Noo-noo, who gazed at her with concern.

"Sorry," she said, reaching out to rub the little dog. "I guess I must have been dreaming. It wasn't a particularly nice dream, apparently."

She headed into the kitchen to pour herself a glass of water. In the process, she realized why she always tried never to go to the store without a list. They'd forgotten paper towels and napkins, which were both big reasons why they'd needed to go to the store in the first place. Beatrice groaned. After the delightfully quiet afternoon, she had no desire to go to the store. But she also had no desire to ask Wyatt to go.

It would be a quick trip, she decided. In and out. She'd head right for the aisle with all the paper products on it, checkout, and then leave. No lollygagging in the cracker aisle.

But when she walked into Bub's Grocery, she was immediately assailed by the sound of an argument in progress. On closer inspection, it appeared Tiggy was giving Harlowe a piece of her mind.

Chapter Seventeen

Beatrice steered her cart toward them. "Is everything okay?"

Harlowe looked at her with relief. "Beatrice."

Tiggy, however, looked close to tears. "I was just letting Harlowe know he needed to tell people that Dan does good work. No matter what Summer said. He works really hard and does a wonderful job with everything he takes on. Summer just expected way too much."

A couple of tears slid down Tiggy's cheek.

Beatrice said in a calm voice, "Okay. I know you're upset, Tiggy. But I think you also know Harlowe hasn't done anything. It isn't Harlowe you're angry with, is it?"

Tiggy stiffened and looked as if she was going to spit out an angry retort. But then her thin shoulders slumped, and she shook her head miserably.

Harlowe said, "Tiggy, I'm real sorry about what Summer said. I know Dan did a good job—Summer wouldn't have hired him in the first place if he hadn't been an excellent contractor. I know she wasn't being fair to him."

"He was doing the best he could," said Tiggy in a scratchy voice. "He had other jobs to work on, not just hers."

"Summer had been a bit more short-tempered than usual while overseeing the studio's construction," acknowledged Harlowe. "Not just with Dan, but with me, too. She just wanted everything to be perfect. She had a real vision for the space and didn't want anything to interfere with her vision or the timing of it. I'm sorry about what happened."

Tiggy started crying in earnest then. "And I'm sorry I'm still so mad at Summer. She's dead and I shouldn't still feel mad at her. I feel really guilty about that."

Beatrice said, "Tiggy, I think that's only natural. Dan is still experiencing ramifications from what was said."

"Right now, he's still not getting any jobs, especially since people are wondering if he's a suspect."

Harlowe said in a quiet voice, "I promise I'll help out. I'll try to spread the word that Dan was doing a great job and that nobody could live up to Summer's expectations at that time."

Tiggy nodded. "Thank you. I'm so sorry I yelled at you." She looked around her at the grocery store and turned a bright pink. "I don't know what people must think of me."

Beatrice said stoutly, "They think you care about Dan and want to help him out."

Tiggy nodded again and said, "Thanks, you two. And sorry again." With that, she took her cart and hastily headed off in another direction.

Harlowe exhaled. "Thanks, Beatrice. I wasn't sure what to do to help her calm down." He rubbed his face. Then he looked at Beatrice and said slowly, "I hate to ask this, but you don't think Tiggy could have had anything to do with Summer's death, do you? I know she and Dan have been seeing each other for a while. Maybe she just lost her temper when she was with Summer."

Beatrice pictured frowsy, skinny Tiggy. She could get indignant, but she was no killer. "No, not at all. She's just standing up for Dan, that's all."

"Yeah, but she's really angry. You should have heard her before you came up. What if she went to the studio that morning to confront Summer and just lost her temper? Things can happen when you're really mad, you know? She could have seen red and attacked Summer."

Beatrice shook her head. "Sorry, I just can't see it."

Harlowe slumped. "You're probably right. I've just been wracking my brains trying to figure out who might have done this. I'm not going to get any real closure until there's justice for Summer. You know, I can't believe how much I miss her."

"It must be hard," said Beatrice softly. "You two were together since college."

"Exactly. I mean, I miss her on one level . . . she was my wife and we used to bounce thoughts and ideas off each other all the time. But I miss her on another level, too . . . just the day-to-day routines. All of my days were structured around her. We'd have coffee together in the mornings and talk about what we thought our days would be like. We even tried to take our lunch breaks at the same time so we could talk on the phone with each other during them." He sighed. "That studio has caused me a whole lot of grief. First when it was being constructed and now when it's the place where Summer was taken from me."

"Have you decided what's going to happen to it? It sounded like you weren't really sure before what your plans were."

"I think I'm going to move ahead with it. It's such a specific type of building that it's not like it can really be used for anything but exercise. But being in there makes me sad. I'm going to rent it out . . . I don't want to be involved in it."

Beatrice said, "I can totally understand that. And I think you have a good idea. There's really not a place in Dappled Hills that's just for exercising. I'll be interested in hearing what programs start up there."

They chatted a bit more for a couple of minutes and then headed off their separate ways. Beatrice rued the fact she'd gotten a shopping cart because she proceeded to fill it with impulse buys on her way over to the paper goods aisle. The next time, she promised herself, she wouldn't go shopping when she was hungry.

A couple of days passed quietly by in the usual way. Beatrice finished her book and did some quilting. Wyatt got a bit further ahead on writing sermons.

One afternoon, Noo-noo gave her doggy grin at Beatrice and pointed her small body toward her harness which was hanging on a hook on the wall.

Beatrice chuckled. "You're not built like a pointer, but you do a good job letting me know what you want. You're absolutely right—we should go for a walk, shouldn't we? I've been very sedentary the last couple of days."

Beatrice decided that she'd been *so* sedentary (and Noo-noo, too, by default), that they should extend their walk from the neighborhood to the park. They set out to walk, heading downtown. Noo-noo was so happy to stretch her legs that she didn't spend much time sniffing at all the fascinating things that were calling out to her on the side of the sidewalk.

As they walked, a couple of folks waved from their cars and Beatrice waved back as Noo-noo grinned. The sun felt warm on her, but there was a light breeze that made the day comfortable.

They reached the park, and then they started around the circumference of it. It was the corgi's favorite walk because there were lots of kids to watch and people to say hi to as they strolled through. Several were from the church and Beatrice chatted to them for a few minutes before they continued on.

They'd just reached the far end of the park when Beatrice spotted Quinn with a big cup of coffee and a black lab on a leash. She smiled at him and he immediately came over.

Noo-noo quickly got on her back at the sight of the bigger dog and Beatrice chuckled. "She knows when to throw in the towel."

Quinn gave her a tired smile. "Ranger is a sweet guy, I promise."

Soon Noo-noo apparently decided he was, too, because she stood back up so Ranger and she could visit properly.

"Beautiful dog," said Beatrice.

"Thanks. I'm thankful Tobi didn't take him," said Quinn wryly. "He was my dog before I started dating Tobi, but she loved him as much as I do."

"Well, I'm glad to see you out and about. You look a bit better."

He gave her a rueful smile. "Do you think so? I realized nobody was going to rescue me from the predicament I put myself in. Tobi has told me she intends to file for divorce."

Beatrice managed a look of surprise, although she'd known from her talk with Tobi that divorce sounded very likely. "I'm so sorry, Quinn."

Quinn took a deep breath. "I know I screwed up. I'm going to spend this time apart by trying to get my life back together.

Tobi must have really been fed up to want a divorce. She says she wants to go back to school and become a teacher." He shook his head in amazement. "She's sort of inspiring me to pick myself up, brush myself off, and jump back into life. I need to fix what's broken."

"That's a great attitude."

He snorted. "Better than the one I had a few days ago. I think I was just bent on self-destruction." He paused, taking a sip of coffee before saying, "I did talk to Wyatt and he really helped me see things in a different perspective."

Beatrice realized that Wyatt must have spoken to both Quinn and Tobi separately. Tobi had planned on speaking with him, too.

"Oh, I'm glad you met with him. Wyatt is great for that."

Quinn nodded. "I'm going to take this time to focus on myself for a while. Although part of me *does* want to jump into another relationship. That's always been my way, though, so I figure I should do something different. I've always found somebody on the rebound and it never ends up working out. Plus, it's not fair to whoever I'm dating."

"That makes a lot of sense."

He said slowly, "Although there's one woman who I've been interested in dating for a long while. She's never seemed like she was available before, but I understand she might be now. You probably know her—she works at the library."

"Remi, perhaps? She's about your age, I think."

Quinn nodded. "That's right. At some point, if she's still available later, I'd love to ask her out. I'm a big reader, myself, and we always have these great conversations about books."

"She's been giving me all kinds of great stuff to read. Remi can even group books by tone and hand me selections that fit my mood. She's a great resource at the library. So you're thinking about asking her out?"

Quinn said, "Of course I want to, but I'm willing to wait. I have the feeling it's just not the best thing to do now. If I try to date someone right this minute, with the mess I've been, they'll probably end up breaking up with me within a week. I'm kind of a wreck."

He continued with a short laugh, "I can't even promise I won't go to jail at the end of the day. How can a person possibly start a relationship with someone when they might end up going to prison for murder? Ramsay has been asking me about the old woman who lived next door to Summer. I never even noticed her."

"Wasn't Ramsay just following up? As a matter of routine?"

Quinn shook his head. "He seemed pretty serious to me. He said Sylvia had told him before she died that she'd seen me at Summer's house the morning she died."

Beatrice caught her breath.

Quinn said in a rush, "But she totally got her dates wrong. I'd been at Summer's house the day *before* she died. Besides, the whole reason I went over to Summer's place to begin with was to tell her it was over."

"Weren't you worried about Harlowe when you went over there?"

Quinn said, "Of course, but I was trying to be really cautious. Believe me, I didn't want to have to be there at all. The problem was that Summer wasn't answering my texts or calls. If she had, I definitely never would have been there." He sighed. "I wish I'd never gone over there; it's causing me nothing but trouble. I should have just sent her a text message telling her that our relationship was over. And now I can't set the record straight because she's dead."

Quinn continued, "Summer and I actually got along really well until we suddenly didn't. And regardless of how messy ending a relationship with her was, I'd never have lifted a finger toward her."

He glanced toward the front of the park and frowned. "Oh no."

Beatrice turned and saw Ramsay walking toward them. Noo-noo greeted Ramsay when he came up to them and he stooped to pet the little dog. Ranger hung back a little, perhaps worried about his owner's obvious reticence.

Chapter Eighteen

"Saw your truck parked here and thought I'd come up for a little talk," Ramsay said to Quinn.

Quinn's posture became immediately defensive. "Okay."

"You see, the problem was that although you said you were at Summer's house the day before she died, it must have been the day of."

Quinn started shaking his head halfway through Ramsay's sentence. "No. It was the day before."

"You see, you mentioned a downed tree to someone and the fact that you were worried Summer was in a bad mood because of it. But that tree came down the morning Summer died."

Quinn's forehead crinkled and Beatrice wondered if he was trying to figure out who he'd spoken with about the downed tree. She hoped he didn't remember it was Remi.

He slumped. "Okay. It's true. I was there to see Summer the morning she died. The only reason I didn't tell the truth is because I knew you'd never believe me."

Ramsay's posture indicated he wasn't even sure he was believing him then. "Go on."

Quinn took a deep breath. "I went over to Summer's house to break up with her, just like I said. It was very early in the morning and she hadn't been answering my emails or any of my texts."

"So you walked inside and told her you wanted to break off the relationship. She got angry, things got out of control, and you killed her." Ramsay's eyes were cold.

Quinn said in a panic, "No! Nothing like that. When I walked into the studio, Summer was already dead. I figured it would look bad if I were at the scene, so I took off. Besides, I needed to head back home before Tobi realized I'd left."

Ramsay pressed his lips together.

"It's true," said Quinn desperately. "I know I should have called the police. Believe me, I feel ashamed at just leaving. But you can see where it was going to cause a ton of problems for me if I stuck around and called you. You'd be saying I killed Summer in a moment of passion. And I *didn't*."

Ramsay considered him thoughtfully. "Okay, let's say, for the sake of argument, what you're saying is true. Did you see anyone around the studio when you were arriving or leaving? Other cars? Anyone in the shadows? Any sort of clue as to who might have done this?"

"When I was arriving there, I was being really cautious because I didn't want to be seen. I looked around me carefully, even though I didn't think any of Summer's fitness clients would be there that early. I was also keeping an eye out for Harlowe. I didn't see anyone. Then, after I'd found Summer's body, I was just trying to get out of there as fast as I could. I was so intent on getting away that I didn't really pay a lot of attention."

Ramsay looked down to write a couple of notes on his notepad. Beatrice noticed Quinn look surprised for a second before he quickly resumed a more neutral expression. She wondered if maybe he did remember something. Whatever it was, Quinn decided not to share it.

Ramsay tapped his pen against his notepad. "How *do* you think Summer would have reacted? If you'd been able to speak with her and told her you wanted to break up with her?"

"I'd been steeling myself because I didn't think Summer would have reacted well at all. But there was ultimately nothing she could do—she couldn't force me to continue the affair."

Ramsay nodded. "Okay. Well, that's all I need for now. I know where to find you if I have any other questions. Beatrice, good to see you." He stooped to say goodbye to Noo-noo before heading back toward his police cruiser. Quinn's dog gave Ramsay a wary look as he left.

As Ramsay took off, Quinn said, "See? That's exactly why I didn't tell him I'd found Summer before you did. Now he's sure I did it."

"If Ramsay were sure, he'd have arrested you."

Quinn looked slightly relieved at this. "I guess that's true."

Beatrice paused and then said carefully, "For a second, when you were speaking with Ramsay, I thought maybe you'd remembered something."

"What?" Quinn gave a startled laugh. "Maybe you're thinking about the moment when I realized I hadn't paid the water bill. Tobi used to take care of a lot of household stuff and I'm really struggling to fill her shoes. Anyway, I'll need to pay that and a couple of other bills once I get back to the house. Which means I better get this walk with Ranger finished and then head back home. I'll see you later, Beatrice."

He and Ranger headed off toward the trail leading to a mountain hike. Noo-noo looked at Beatrice as if asking when they were going to continue the fun walk they'd been having.

She reached down to scratch Noo-noo behind her large ears. "Ready to walk?"

They continued their stroll through the park, stopping a couple of times as children with their parents would ask if they could pet the corgi. Noo-noo wagged her nubbin of a tail and looked as if she was having the best day ever.

Then they headed back to the house. It took a bit longer this time because Noo-noo was now ready to smell various tempting spots along the way. When they finally reached the house, Beatrice was fumbling to find her front door key when she heard her name being called. She turned to see Savannah waving at her and coming up on her bike.

"We're popular today, Noo-noo," murmured Beatrice.

Savannah grinned at her as she leaned her bike against a tree. "Hi there, Beatrice. How are things?"

"Oh, pretty well. Are you out doing errands or getting exercise?"

Savannah said, "Just killing time, actually. I finished organizing all my craft items and then felt as if I needed to get out of the house for a while."

Beatrice doubted that Savannah's craft items actually needed tidying or organizing at all. She was one of the most organized people she knew.

"Want to come inside for a visit, then? I can help you kill time for a while," said Beatrice.

Savannah was delighted to do so. And Beatrice was glad that she'd tidied up a bit in the morning before she'd left the house.

Cammie came running up to join them, giving Savannah an austere look through the locks of hair over her eyes.

Savannah said, "Who's this?" She sat on the sofa and reached down to pick up the little dog. But Cammie wasn't having it. She looked at Savannah reproachfully and backed her small body up, giving some yippy barks at Savannah to let her know she'd stepped out of line.

"Goodness," said Savannah with a bemused frown. "I think I've offended her."

Beatrice said, "This is Cammie. She was Sylvia's dog. You might have seen her coming out of Sylvia's purse when they were out and about. And I don't think you've offended her at all . . . she just likes taking things slow."

Savannah reached out a hand and Cammie gave her a suspicious look before cautiously coming up to sniff it.

"I didn't know Sylvia," said Savanah. "I knew who she *was*, of course, and I saw her in Posy's shop a few times, but I never spoke to her. I never even noticed she had a dog. Are you going to keep her?"

Beatrice shook her head. "No, I'm just fostering her for a while until she finds a forever home. Meadow is thinking about taking her in."

Savannah's eyes widened. "You're kidding. Boris will eat her alive."

Beatrice chuckled. "I can't believe I'm saying this, but Boris *loves* her."

"Because she's tasty?" Savannah looked worried.

"No, because he thinks she's wonderful. He's very calm around Cammie. Meadow thinks Cammie may be a balm for his soul."

Savannah reached out her hand again, this time to pet Cammie. Cammie still looked dubious, but allowed Savannah to reach out and gently pet her fur. Savannah asked, "What does Ramsay think?"

"I'm not sure Meadow has broached the subject of them adopting Cammie yet. She'll probably wait until after Ramsay's investigation is finished. He's really under the gun now, with two murders to solve. Introducing a new dog into his household is the last thing on his mind." Beatrice stood up. "And look at me, forgetting my manners. Can I get you something to drink?"

"Oh, a glass of ice water would be great," said Savannah. She sat on the sofa and started loving on Noo-noo, who appeared to be absolutely eating it up.

Beatrice brought in the water and sat down across from Savannah. "By the way, I loved what you did with Meadow's crazy quilt."

Savannah winced a bit at the mention of the quilt. "Thanks, Beatrice. It was a little outside of my *milieu*. But I suppose it turned out all right."

"What quilt are you working on now that the UFO project is done?"

Beatrice strongly suspected she knew the answer to the question before she'd even asked it. Savannah, naturally, would be working on a geometric print of some sort.

Savannah quickly warmed to her subject. "It's a modern quilt pattern."

She looked at Beatrice for approval, and Beatrice quickly nodded her head. "That sounds like fun. What sort of modern pattern?"

As expected, it turned out to be a modern take on a log cabin geometric print. Savannah said, "I'm making it with three different colored prints. I felt like I could take on a big challenge right now and it's a king-sized quilt. How about you?"

Beatrice made a face. "My quilting is something of a mess right now. I'm so distracted by other things that I'm not focusing on what I'm doing. Apparently, I can't chew bubblegum and walk at the same time."

"You've been thinking about Summer?" asked Savannah. "And Sylvia?" Cammie came up closer to Savannah, studying her. Then she put her little feet up on Savannah's legs.

Savannah's eyes opened wider. "Does she want me to pick her up?"

"It's looking that way," said Beatrice with a grin.

Savannah reached down and gently picked up the tiny dog. Cammie looked at her solemnly and then settled down on her lap. Savannah carefully stroked her on the head and Cammie almost looked as if she'd suddenly purr with pleasure.

"Are you sure *you* don't want to take Cammie home?" asked Beatrice teasingly.

Savannah looked rueful. "I would. I certainly would. But Mr. Smoke would not be amused."

Mr. Smoke was Savannah's gray cat. A gray cat that was very used to having his very own sunbeams and routine. A routine that decidedly didn't include a small dog named Cammie.

"I can imagine that," said Beatrice. "But then, Smoke is just not used to any other animals. And, sorry, you asked me a question. What was it, again?"

"Oh, I was just asking if Summer and Sylvia had been on your mind a lot. You were saying you were distracted."

Beatrice said ruefully, "You can see how distracted I've been. And Summer and Sylvia have definitely been on my mind, yes."

"I've been thinking about them, too," said Savannah. "Mostly because Dan is being blamed for their deaths. I'm glad Meadow and Posy are setting up that silent auction. You know how Dan is—he doesn't say a word about how awful he feels or how worried he is about getting surgery. He just keeps plugging along."

"I hope the auction will raise a lot for him. It's got to be on his mind all the time. Maybe the town will start to forget what Summer said. Everyone who's hired Dan knows he runs his projects on time and that he does a fantastic job." Beatrice paused. "Dan hasn't found out about the fundraiser, has he?"

Savannah shook her head. "Fortunately not. Like Meadow was saying, it's better if someone from the Village Quilters presents him with a check after the fact so he doesn't find out in advance and shut us down." Savannah sighed. "And It will help him get work once the murderer is caught and taken to jail. I really hope Ramsay can figure out who's behind this so he can get on with business as usual."

"I'm sure he's making some good progress. You know how Ramsay throws everything into his cases. Did you know Summer at all, thinking of the murders?" There was no one she could think of who was a less-likely candidate for attending fitness classes than Savannah.

Savannah held up a spindly finger. "Actually, I know quite a bit *of* her. But no, I never really spoke to her."

"What have you heard about her?"

Savannah drew closer, as if someone might overhear them in Beatrice's living room. "She was giving out investment advice. Can you believe it? I thought it was a totally irresponsible thing to do."

Beatrice frowned. "Are you sure we're talking about the same person? Summer wasn't a licensed stockbroker or financial advisor."

Savannah nodded. "Exactly. That was my reaction. Who takes investment advice from a fitness coach?"

"But people did?"

Savannah said, "The thing was that Summer was apparently doing very well on the stock market. I guess she was one of those lucky people. Some people just seem to have a really good radar when it comes to choosing stocks. Like I say, she was lucky."

"Until she wasn't."

Savannah grimaced. "Yes. Until she came to a terrible end. Anyway, she had some money to invest, and she ended up putting it into stocks that ended up doing very well." She paused. "Maybe it wasn't that she was lucky. Perhaps she did put some time into researching things. Whether it was luck or research, she made a good deal of money. But other people, following her advice, lost money. I use her story as a cautionary tale for my clients."

Savannah was an accountant and Beatrice had no doubt she was a very good one. And, perhaps, a very cautious one. She was the kind of person who liked t's crossed and i's dotted. If Savannah were doing your taxes, there was no way you'd get into trouble with the IRS.

"This seems like the kind of thing Ramsay should know," said Beatrice slowly. "If someone lost a lot of money, they could have been angry enough at Summer to take revenge. Do you know who the person was? Or people?"

Savannah shook her head. "No." She frowned. "You think I should call Ramsay?"

"Definitely. He can figure out if it's useful information or not."

Savannah said, "I'll do that, then."

Talk moved on to other, milder, topics, centering mainly on Savannah's cat, Cammie, and Noo-noo, since Savannah was a real animal lover. Georgia had apparently made Savannah some cute bowties for Smoke and she was thinking Maisie the shop cat might like one of Georgia's bows. Then Savannah took her leave, carefully putting Cammie on the floor before heading out on her bike, reiterating that she'd contact Ramsay as soon as she got back home.

Alone again, Beatrice tried to figure out what she wanted to do next for her day. Ordinarily, she'd prefer quietly working on her quilt or reading her book. But she had the sinking sensation that both she and Wyatt were going to run out of clean clothes unless she went ahead and tackled the laundry. She pulled together a load of whites and collected some hangers so that she could hang up the shirts right after they came out of the dryer. She was starting the load when her phone rang.

Wyatt said, "Just wanted to give you a heads-up that Quinn has had some sort of accident. I know you've spoken with him lately and just wanted to fill you in."

Chapter Nineteen

"An accident? What sort of accident?"

Wyatt said, "Apparently, he must have had something on his mind and was distracted. He ran off the road and hit a tree."

"Oh no. Is he very hurt?" Beatrice couldn't imagine anyone having a collision with a tree and *not* being very hurt.

"He's not in great shape. Quinn has a lot of contusions and fractures. But considering how bad he *could* have been, it seems almost as if he was lucky."

Beatrice said, "Is he in the hospital?"

"He's not been admitted, no. They patched him up and sent him back home."

Beatrice made a face. "If his house was in bad shape before, it's sure to be in terrible shape now that he can't really even tidy it up. I should bring him some food."

"I think the congregational care committee is already planning to bring meals by."

"Just the same, I'll pop over there. Maybe I can give him a hand with something else. It sounds like he could use a housekeeper."

Wyatt chuckled. "Don't get sucked in. It sounds like there might be more mess over there than you'll want to deal with."

After Beatrice hung up, she decided to pick up a fried chicken dinner and, remembering the fact he often seemed to have a large coffee nearby, a big container of coffee for Quinn. It sounded like an opportunity to speak with him again, besides just helping out with meals. She hopped in the car, picked up the chicken and sides, and headed over to Quinn's house.

On the way, she mulled over what Savannah had told her earlier. There was something she was missing there, and she was determined to figure out what it was. Something about a person losing money on the stock market. Then she slowly realized what had been bothering her. Remi had fallen on hard times lately. Of course, librarians didn't make very much to begin with, but Remi had never had to use church resources before. Remi had also been friends with Summer before that had abruptly broken off. What if Remi had been the person who'd gotten bad investment advice from Summer? That could have been the final straw. Remi was already annoyed that Summer hadn't reached out to Quinn for her. If she'd given Remi rotten recommendations that had made her lose money, that would have been even worse.

Another realization suddenly jolted her. Piper had mentioned Remi had been to Summer's house. But Remi had claimed never to have been there. She'd stated she'd just driven by on her way to work each day. It could be that Remi had simply forgotten she'd been at Summer's house, but it was enough of an anomaly that Beatrice felt she shouldn't keep the information to herself.

Beatrice pulled into Quinn's driveway and called Ramsay. His phone rang and rang, but he didn't answer. She figured he might be on the phone with Savannah, since she'd promised she'd call him.

Beatrice left a message, "Hi, Ramsay. Could you give me a call back? I've noticed some inconsistencies with Remi."

Her phone rang, and she thought Ramsay had gotten her message and was calling her back. But it was Meadow.

"Guess what? Ramsay would like us to take in Cammie." Meadow's voice was bouncy and Beatrice could imagine that Meadow was just as bouncy wherever she was. "I wasn't going to bring anything up until after this investigation was over, but he brought it up himself! He said he thought part of Boris's problem was he needed another dog to hang out with. That Boris, even with all the attention he gets from us, could use a canine companion. I mean, we play ball with Boris outside, but we end up tired when he's still raring to go. And he always wins the tug-of-war game with his favorite rope. He has a lot more energy than we do. Maybe he just needs a furry friend. Besides that, I love Cammie, too. It would be awesome to have a dog small enough to sit on my lap."

"You don't think Boris will be jealous of Cammie?"

"Oh, I don't think so. I've held Cammie on my lap the last couple of times I've been over and Boris didn't blink an eye."

"Wonderful!" said Beatrice. "I think you'll find Cammie is a great little girl. She has perfect manners." Unlike Boris, who never seemed to realize he needed to ask for treats instead of taking them for himself.

Meadow said, "How about if I pick her up later this afternoon? Do you think she'll have a tough time adjusting to being in a new place?"

"I don't think so. Cammie seems like she sort of takes life as it comes. Ramsay had picked up all her things from Sylvia's house and brought them over: her bed, her toys, and things like that. Those have made a big difference in helping her get used to being over here and I'll pass them along to you when you come by." Beatrice paused. "By the way, is Ramsay over there? I was trying to get in touch with him. Something I realized about the case."

Meadow's voice got even more excited, if that were possible. "You mean you've figured something out? The investigation is finally going to close up?"

"Well, I'm not sure that's entirely true, no. It's just something that I thought was a bit of an aberration, that's all. If he happens to get in touch with you before he reaches out to me, could you pass along the message?"

"Of course I will! I can't wait to get rid of a Dappled Hills bad guy." She paused. "You're not tracking him down *yourself*, though, Beatrice, are you?"

"I thought that's what you wanted me to do," said Beatrice wryly.

"Certainly not! I only wanted you to connect the dots, entirely in your head. More like a Nero Wolfe who just sits around reading and taking care of his orchids while solving the mystery. You don't need to act like Nancy Drew and chase the person *down*. Leave that to the professionals."

Beatrice smiled. "It sounds as if you're all too willing to put Ramsay in danger."

"Let me remind you that Ramsay is a police chief. He has a gun. You're an unarmed quilter and retired art museum curator."

Beatrice said, "I'll put your mind at rest; I'm most assuredly *not* chasing criminals right now. All I'm doing is delivering food to Quinn. It sounds as if he might be homebound for a while and need a bit of help with meals."

"Gracious, yes. I heard about that. He's had the worst possible luck lately. Well, I'm glad you're bringing some food by to him." Meadow paused. "And you don't think *he's* the murderer, do you? Just checking. Because, in *that* case, you'd be putting yourself in danger again, which is precisely what we don't want."

"I don't believe so, no. I know he wasn't happy with Summer because she didn't want to end the relationship, but somehow, I just can't see him killing her. Of course, even if he were the murderer, my understanding is that he's pretty much incapacitated right now."

Meadow was quiet for a second. "I was just thinking about you being Nancy Drew."

"Sadly, I think I'm a little older than Nancy. Wasn't she eighteen? And she drove a blue roadster? I was never entirely clear what a roadster was, but it sounded very cool."

Meadow said, "Nancy isn't bound by years, Beatrice. After all, she was eighteen in 1930. By that standard, she'd be quite a bit older than us."

"Or something."

"Anyway, if you were Nancy Drew, would I be Bess or George?" asked Meadow.

"Oh, I think you'd be Bess, wouldn't you? George was a tomboy."

"Good point, Beatrice. I rather like the idea of being Bess. Although she was a little timid, wasn't she?"

Beatrice said, "Cautious might be the better term for it." She paused. "I'm at Quinn's house now, so I'd better go or he'll be wondering who's lurking in his driveway."

"Lurking in your blue roadster?"

"Or something," said Beatrice again with a laugh. "Talk to you later."

She walked toward the front door with the chicken dinner and coffee in hand. As she got closer to the house, she could hear a female voice raised inside.

Chapter Twenty

Beatrice paused. Was Tobi inside, arguing with Quinn? The last thing she wanted to do was to interrupt some sort of domestic argument. But Tobi's car wasn't parked outside. Besides, she couldn't really picture Tobi coming over to Quinn's house to argue with him. She'd gotten the impression the last time she spoke with Tobi that she was truly washing her hands of him and was perfectly content in the rental place and moving along with her plans to become a teacher. That she had no interest in squabbling with Quinn over small things. Just the same, she could have come by out of a genuine sense of concern following his accident. But would she be yelling at him as the female voice seemed to be?

Beatrice hesitated and then moved closer to the door.

Quinn said flatly, "I know it was you, Remi. Ramsay asked me recently if I remembered anything from when I found Summer. All I've been thinking about is whether anyone spotted *me* and might tell the cops I was around. Once I thought about it again, I did recall something else that had nothing to do with me. I remember your car was parked some distance away, and you weren't in it. I noticed that before I found Summer. After I saw her body lying there, everything else was temporarily wiped out of my mind."

Beatrice's heart was beating hard inside her chest as she leaned even closer to the door. Remi had done it? Really done it. She carefully put her phone on vibrate. If Ramsay called her back, she didn't want the ringing to alert Remi that she was there.

Remi's voice was shrill as she answered, "You remembered my car was in the area and decided to turn me in. Is that it?"

"Like I said on the phone, I just wanted to find out if there was a reasonable explanation for your car being where it was. You and I have always had a connection, Remi. You know, I was even thinking about asking you out. I wanted to at least give you the courtesy of the benefit of the doubt. As far as I knew, you could have been visiting Sylvia next door . . . checking on her or something. You could even have been delivering her a library book on your way to work. I mean, it would have been a pretty early visit, but anything was possible. Or maybe you had broken down and had gotten a ride home from somebody."

Remi said in a dull voice, "I just ran out of gas. That's why you saw my car there. I don't take much notice of car maintenance. I caught a ride out there later with a gas can and filled it up enough to get to the station to fill it up the rest of the way."

"I don't think so, Remi. You've been acting funny ever since you showed up here. You were the one who killed Summer, weren't you? The thing I don't get is why. Why would you have done that? I thought you and Summer were good friends."

Beatrice texted Ramsay an update, afraid of calling him and being overheard. Then, worried for Quinn's safety, she slipped inside the unlocked front door. She passed through the foyer and to the edge of the living room, where Quinn and Remi were speaking.

Remi's voice was shrill again. "Summer didn't know how to be a friend. Friends don't treat friends the way she treated me."

Quinn said sadly, "I thought *you and I* were friends. But here you are, pointing a gun at me."

An icy tingle rose up Beatrice's spine. She wrapped her fingers tightly around the steaming hot jumbo coffee she was carrying.

Remi said, "Sorry, Quinn. I can't have you telling the cops about this."

Beatrice rushed into the room and flung the contents of the coffee cup on Remi.

Remi screamed and fumbled with the gun.

Quinn, with bandages all over his injured body, tried to grab the gun, but Remi was able to regain control of it.

Remi turned, fuming, and pointed the gun at Beatrice. "Get over there next to him." Her eyes were full of fury.

Beatrice slowly walked over to sit next to Quinn on the sofa. He gave her an apologetic look. Beatrice reached out and squeezed his hand. "It's okay, Quinn."

Quinn whispered, "I'd never have called Remi if I'd known. I can't believe it's her. That's why I wanted to give her a chance to explain before I phoned Ramsay."

Remi aimed the gun at both of them. "That's enough talking."

"Where did you get the gun?" asked Beatrice as if she were politely inquiring over a fetching new dress.

Remi said, "It's not such a weird thing to own. I grew up around here, you know. My granddad raised me and taught me how to shoot. He also gave me this gun. So don't worry; I know my way around a weapon."

"I don't think your grandfather would approve of the way you're using it now, Remi," said Beatrice grimly.

The hand holding the gun wavered slightly, but was still pointed directly at Beatrice and Quinn. She said, "You don't know what my grandfather would have liked or disliked."

Beatrice said, "I have the feeling he cared about you and wouldn't want you to show such disrespect for life. And for your friends. Because, think of it. Quinn and I both considered ourselves friends."

Another slight waver with the gun. Remi shook her head. "You don't really know me, Beatrice. You just know me from work."

Quinn gave Beatrice a desperate look, egging her on to talk more. Maybe, if she could keep Remi talking, she could reason with her and buy them some time. She didn't have much hope for Quinn being able to do anything to defend them, though. Judging from what she could see, he had far too many fractures to really be able to help them out.

"Being a librarian is a little more than just work, isn't it? It's like sharing a favorite hobby with someone else. I really treasured the way you'd feel out my mood and help me find a novel that you'd also enjoyed. It was a connection, wasn't it?"

Beatrice hoped Remi would remember and feel that connection again. The way she was staring at her with those blank eyes gave her the chills. It was almost as if Remi had already relegated them to death.

She was relieved to see a bit more emotion in Remi's eyes. Remi said, "Reading is an escape, but it can't help us escape *everything.* You both know I can't just let you walk out of here, don't you?"

Quinn quickly said, "But you can. Like Beatrice was saying, we're all friends. At least, Beatrice and I consider you a friend, even if it's not vice-versa. That's why I made the phone call that got you here to begin with. And Remi—you can't believe that you're going to get away with this now. Two dead bodies in my house?"

"I can move you," said Remi in a dead voice that gave Beatrice the chills.

"No way," said Quinn, sounding a bit more confident than he had earlier. "Maybe you could lug Beatrice a little bit, but there's no way you can move me. Plus, I have people coming in and out of here all the time checking on me. It's why Beatrice was here to begin with. All sorts of folks from the church are going to come by to bring food and see if they can help me out. They'll find Beatrice and me."

"And with a total of four victims, the search is really going to go into overdrive," said Beatrice. "You're not going to get away with this, Remi. The smartest thing to do is realize that it's over and turn yourself in. You'll probably get a reduced sentence that way, too." Beatrice had absolutely no idea if that was true, but at this point, she was going to say anything to try and get out of this.

But Remi's face remained hard and determined. "You can talk all day long, but you're not going to convince me. I've gotten away with this so far and I'm planning on keeping it that way."

"The neighbors will hear gunshots," said Quinn quickly. "They'll come over and see what's happened."

"Then I'll shoot them, too." Remi's voice was completely devoid of emotion. She levelled the gun at them. Quinn gave Beatrice's hand a squeeze.

Which was when the familiar strains of *Joyful, Joyful, We Adore Thee* came from behind them as a cell phone rang at full volume.

Chapter Twenty-One

Remi whirled around, gasping. As she did, Beatrice struck her from behind as hard as she could with the chicken dinner. Remi's grip loosened on the gun and Beatrice grabbed it from her. Unfamiliar with weapons, she shuttled it over to Quinn, who leveled it at Remi.

When the cell phone guy walked in with a cheerful, "Helloooo?" he froze, stunned, gaping at the sight of Quinn training the gun at Remi, fried chicken and coffee all over the floor, and the minister's wife right in the middle of it.

Beatrice had never been so grateful to see anyone in her life.

Ramsay had finally checked his messages, spoken to Meadow, or both, and was on the scene moments later, followed quickly by the state police. The cell phone guy (Beatrice realized she should think of him as Ace, instead) briefly gave a statement to Ramsay, set the food from the care committee in the fridge, and hastily vacated the premises. Beatrice promised herself she'd never roll her eyes at his ringing phone again.

"What's happened here, Remi?" asked Ramsay, looking grim.

Remi shook her head. "I'm not going to speak with you or any of the other cops. I want to talk with a lawyer.

Ramsay nodded. One of the officers from the state police formally arrested Remi and took her to the station.

Ramsay glanced around the living room. Beatrice noticed that the addition of fried chicken and coffee definitely made the already-messy house look even worse, if that were even possible.

Quinn said, "We can sit in the kitchen, if that's better, Ramsay. I know it's a wreck in here. I'll just need a hand getting off the sofa."

"No, no. You just stay put. Beatrice and I can make this work, can't we?"

Beatrice nodded and sat in a chair across from Quinn and next to Ramsay. Her heart was still pounding so hard that she didn't trust herself to speak.

Ramsay studied both of them. "Are you two okay? It looks like a lot happened here. Do we need to get an ambulance for you?"

Beatrice shook her head, still feeling shaky.

Quinn said wryly, "Please, no more hospitals. I'm bandaged up enough." He gestured to his collection of injuries. Although his tone was light, his face was ashen.

Ramsay nodded. "I hear that. Okay, which of you wants to start out with the recap?"

Quinn and Beatrice looked at each other. "You should go ahead," said Quinn. "Maybe hearing you talk about it will help me to get it straight in my head. My mind is still spinning."

Beatrice took a deep breath. "Well, I guess it started when I spoke with Remi. She'd said in passing that she'd never been to Summer's house. But Piper mentioned to me later that she had."

Ramsay said, "One of those inconsistencies you mentioned in your message."

"Right. But, you know—I figured that maybe Remi had forgotten she'd been to Summer's house or that Piper could have been wrong. Things got a bit more muddled when I was talking with Savannah. She told me Summer had been very successful on the stock market and had been handing out investment advice to people."

Ramsay quirked an eyebrow. "I'm sure Savannah didn't think much of that."

"Exactly. She thought stock market advising should be left to the professionals. I guess Summer had either a streak of luck or had really good acumen when it came to stocks. It sounded like people around town liked to get stock tips from her."

Quinn said wryly, "Summer probably enjoyed that. She'd have liked being the community expert on the stock market. And she probably did know exactly what she was doing on there. I'm not saying Summer wasn't lucky, but she also was the kind of person who'd carefully research things before she jumped into them. If she gave bad investment advice, I bet it's because she *wanted* to give bad investment advice."

"That's interesting. I hadn't even considered the fact that she might have given bad advice as a way of messing with people," said Beatrice. "Anyway, I started thinking about Remi's sudden lack of funds and her falling out with Summer. I'd thought Remi was upset with Summer because she'd failed as a go-between."

Quinn frowned. "A go-between?"

"Remi sent Summer on a mission to find out if you might be interested in dating her."

Quinn's eyes opened wide. "Did she? I didn't know anything about that." His expression stated that he was relieved he hadn't dated Remi.

Beatrice nodded. "I guess Remi had always thought there was a connection between the two of you but wasn't confident about acting on it. She asked Summer, who said she was a friend of yours, to reach out to you and see if you might have lunch or a coffee with her or something. Except that Summer didn't do it. She didn't approach you, but she came back to Remi and said that you wanted to just stay friends."

Ramsay said, "At some point, I guess Remi realized Summer hadn't gotten in touch with Quinn? Did Summer tell her that, or was it something Remi just guessed?"

"Remi said she could tell the next time Quinn came into the library that Summer hadn't said anything to him about it. She said Quinn acted just as he usually did and there wasn't any awkwardness between them at all. That's when she suspected Summer might have double-crossed her. Then Quinn and Tobi started dating and got married. And, sometime later, Quinn and Summer had an affair."

Ramsay raised his eyebrows. "So Remi felt double-crossed by Summer a couple of times over. That must have really riled her up."

"I think it made her mad, sure. But not enough to kill some-one," said Beatrice. "Which might have been why I thought she couldn't really have murdered Summer. Missing an opportunity to date someone hardly seemed like a motive for murder."

"And also because killer librarians are pretty rare," said Quinn, his color returning a little.

Beatrice smiled at him. "True. They can be fierce, but are generally non-violent. But then I realized Remi could have been a friend Summer had given investment advice to. Remi seemed to trust Summer. Maybe Summer gave Remi investment advice around the same time she was supposed to be the intermediary between Remi and you. At that point, she still trusted Summer.

She could have been interested in trying to duplicate the success Summer had had on the stock market and buffered her nest egg a bit. If Remi had lost all her savings, that could have been significant enough for her to want revenge."

"Especially considering that she was already upset about the Quinn thing," said Ramsay.

"So I left a message for you, Ramsay, and headed over to see Quinn and deliver some food to him."

Ramsay snorted. "And probably ask Quinn questions."

Beatrice reddened a little. "Probably."

Quinn said fervently, "I'm glad you came over, no matter what the reason was. If you hadn't been here, I'd be dead right now. There's no way, in the condition I'm in right now, that I'd have been able to put up any kind of fight. And when Remi was pointing a gun at me, I realized just how much I wanted to have a fresh start on life." He shivered. "I couldn't believe how cold she looked. Maybe she did have a crush on me before, but she was totally ready to murder me without a second thought to save her own skin."

"So Beatrice, you delivered the food to Quinn." Ramsay's gaze cast over the coffee and chicken mess on the floor again. But Remi was already here when you arrived?"

"I didn't know she was here at first. Her car wasn't here, for one thing."

Ramsay said, "I noticed driving in that her car is parked far away from the house, so Remi couldn't be spotted. So how did you know she was inside?"

"When I got closer to the house, I could hear raised voices. I heard Quinn saying Remi's name and realized what was going on. And I think Quinn should take it from here."

Quinn nodded. "I wondered if Remi had killed Summer because I spotted her car in the vicinity of Summer's house that morning. It was also parked down the road a bit. Like I mentioned to you at the park, I thought everyone would think I'd killed Summer if I called the police. Plus, the fact we'd had an affair would become public knowledge, too. And I didn't particularly want to deal with an angry husband, thinking I'd offed his wife for some reason. I just left."

"Why didn't you mention to me at the park that you knew Remi had been at Summer's house the morning she died?" asked Ramsay.

Quinn spread out his hands. "I'd only just realized at that moment that it had been Remi's car I'd seen. I wanted to get back home and digest that. Anyway, after I found Summer, I wanted to get away from her house as fast as I could, and undetected. I think I was in shock, too. It was awful—finding Summer there like that. She'd always been so alive and vibrant. I couldn't believe she was gone. The rest of the day was sort of a blur. I didn't really remember any details from that morning. At the park, I remembered I'd passed a car on the way out. I realized I'd seen that car at the library before and that it had a library-related bumper sticker on it. I knew it had to be Remi."

"How did she know you suspected her?" asked Ramsay.

"I called her. You have to remember that Remi and I were friends. I'd talk to her at the library whenever I was picking up a book. I didn't want to just give her up to the police if there was a legitimate reason why her car was there. I figured she might have been on her way to work and her car broke down or something. I called her up."

"And she came over," said Ramsay.

"That's right. And I was a little surprised at that, but I figured she just wanted to chat. After all, we were friends, like I said. Maybe we'd talk about books a little and then she'd laugh and tell me about her car trouble. But when she came inside, she looked agitated and edgy. I knew right then that something was up."

"You still let her in the house, though," said Ramsay.

Quinn sighed. "Yeah, I shouldn't have done that. But I didn't really think she was involved. I didn't *want* to believe she was involved. I mean, those were two really ruthless murders. That's why I wanted to give her the chance to explain before I talked to you. I guess I figured I could handle whatever the situation was."

"Maybe you could before your accident, but those injuries were going to slow you down," noted Ramsay. "Plus, you wouldn't have been much use against a gun, whether you'd been in an accident or not."

"I had no idea she was carrying," said Quinn, raising his hands. "I'd never have let her inside if I had."

Ramsay nodded. "You let her in, and she pulled a gun on you right away?"

"No. She seemed like she was trying to figure out exactly what it was that I knew. But then it was pretty obvious that she was the one responsible. Like I said, her face was almost devoid of any emotion. Except anger."

Ramsay said, "Did she talk about the crimes at all? Give any information or details?"

"Not really. Remi did say that she had to kill Sylvia for the same reason—that she knew too much, just like me. It was sort of a warning to let me know she meant business." Quinn gave a slight shiver, thinking about it.

"So Beatrice came over and heard you two arguing," prompted Ramsay.

Quinn said in a fervent voice. "She did. I don't know if was really the both of us arguing; I think it was mainly me sounding increasingly panicked and Remi getting really angry. I'm so thankful Beatrice came by right at that moment. I was feeling really desperate because I knew there was no way I could get out of the situation, especially as broken up as I am right now. Remi had the gun pointed at me and she was deadly serious. There was no way she was planning on letting me leave that room alive."

Beatrice said, "The front door was unlocked, so I slipped inside to see what was going on. I could hear that Quinn was in trouble."

"And it sounded like you needed to intervene? That his life was in danger?"

"I heard Quinn say that Remi had a gun. I knew I had to do something or else Quinn would end up like Summer and Sylvia." Beatrice pointed to the chicken and coffee all over the floor and furniture. "That's what's left of the meal I brought. I flung the coffee at Remi, and Quinn tried to grab the gun. I didn't see anything else around me to use as a weapon."

"Grabbing the gun didn't work out too well," said Quinn ruefully. "It's like Remi had a death grip on that pistol."

Ramsay nodded. "That's when the guy from church came in with the care committee's food, I suppose."

"Ace, yes. I'll never say another bad thing about his phone incessantly ringing in church," vowed Beatrice. "Hearing *Joyful, Joyful, We Adore Thee* surprised Remi enough for us to get out of here alive."

Quinn said, "I think Remi also sort of gave up at that point. She realized there was no way she was going to control three of us."

"I'd like to think hearing a hymn reminded her that what she was about to do wasn't the right thing. But I have to agree with Quinn—it was more as if she just gave up."

Ramsay nodded and put away his notebook. "Got it. Okay, I'll speak with Remi and get her to fill me in the rest of the way. Good job here, Beatrice."

Beatrice said wryly, "Good timing, is more like it."

Quinn fervently thanked her again, but Beatrice waved him off.

Beatrice said, "Quinn, I'm just glad you're okay. It looks like Ace stuck the casseroles in the fridge for you so you can have them whenever you're ready. Is there anything else you need before I head out? Anyone I can call to come over?"

Although Tobi must have been the first person to come to mind, Quinn shook his head. With a rueful smile, he said, "Honestly, now I just want to take a nap. You'd think I'd be too keyed up to be able to sleep, but I'm absolutely exhausted."

"Okay. But I *am* going to clean up this chicken and coffee from the floor."

Quinn quickly tried to dissuade her from doing so, but Beatrice held up a hand. "Nope."

"But the whole house is trashed," said Quinn.

"That may or may not be. But I didn't trash the rest of the house. I'm going to clean up the bit that I did. Besides, I don't think you can even *get* to the floor to pick this stuff up."

Fifteen minutes later, the chicken was in the trash and the stickiness of the coffee was off the floor. Beatrice was able to put her blinders on and not automatically start cleaning up the rest of the mess.

Quinn looked sheepish. "I think you're inspiring me. After I take that nap, I'm going to pick up a little bit."

"Just don't overdo it."

Quinn said, "I'll just clear off some of the surfaces. That'll make things look a lot better." He paused. "Now I really *do* want to turn things around. The fact that I just barely escaped being murdered is probably behind that."

Beatrice nodded. "Definitely. Do you need a hand getting to your room?"

"Just a little help standing up, since it's been a while and I've gotten stiff."

Quinn struggled up with Beatrice's assistance and his crutches.

After that, she took her leave. Beatrice was getting into her car, her mind still whirling, when Wyatt drove up, looking white as a sheet.

"Are you okay?" he asked in a rush as he got out of the car.

"I'm fine. Who told you?"

Wyatt wrapped his arms around her, and she gave him a tight hug. Some of the stress seeped away.

"Meadow did," he murmured into her hair. "Ramsay was at home when he got your message."

Beatrice snorted. "I'm surprised Meadow isn't over here herself."

"Oh, I'm sure she would have been if she hadn't been watching Will."

Beatrice nodded. There was no way Meadow would have brought her precious grandchild into any sort of dangerous situation.

"Are you okay to drive?" asked Wyatt.

"I'm much better now. I've been helping Quinn get situated, and it steadied my nerves. Why don't you just follow me home? I'll pull over if I'm too shaky."

And so he did. Noo-noo eagerly greeted her at the door and Beatrice drew the furry girl close to her, letting her lick her on the neck. Wyatt poured her a glass of white wine and put some soft music on. Back in the safety of the cozy cottage, everything was suddenly right in her world . . . and in Dappled Hills.

About the Author

Elizabeth writes the Southern Quilting mysteries and Memphis Barbeque mysteries for Penguin Random House and the Myrtle Clover series for Midnight Ink and independently. She blogs at ElizabethSpannCraig.com/blog, named by Writer's Digest as one of the 101 Best Websites for Writers. Elizabeth makes her home in Matthews, North Carolina, with her husband. She's the mother of two.

Sign up for Elizabeth's free newsletter to stay updated on releases:

https://bit.ly/2xZUXqO

This and That

I love hearing from my readers. You can find me on Facebook as Elizabeth Spann Craig Author, on Twitter as elizabethscraig, on my website at elizabethspanncraig.com, and by email at elizabethspanncraig@gmail.com.

Thanks so much for reading my book...I appreciate it. If you enjoyed the story, would you please leave a short review on the site where you purchased it? Just a few words would be great. Not only do I feel encouraged reading them, but they also help other readers discover my books. Thank you!

Did you know my books are available in print and ebook formats? Most of the Myrtle Clover series is available in audio and some of the Southern Quilting mysteries are. Find the audiobooks here: https://elizabethspanncraig.com/audio/

Please follow me on BookBub for my reading recommendations and release notifications.

I'd also like to thank some folks who helped me put this book together. Thanks to my cover designer, Karri Klawiter, for her awesome covers. Thanks to my editor, Judy Beatty for her help. Thanks to beta readers Amanda Arrieta, Rebecca Wahr, Cassie Kelley, and Dan Harris for all of their helpful suggestions and careful reading. Thanks to my ARC readers for helping to spread the word. Thanks, as always, to my family and readers.

Other Works by Elizabeth

Myrtle Clover Series in Order (be sure to look for the Myrtle series in audio, ebook, and print):

Pretty is as Pretty Dies

Progressive Dinner Deadly

A Dyeing Shame

A Body in the Backyard

Death at a Drop-In

A Body at Book Club

Death Pays a Visit

A Body at Bunco

Murder on Opening Night

Cruising for Murder

Cooking is Murder

A Body in the Trunk

Cleaning is Murder

Edit to Death

Hushed Up

A Body in the Attic

Murder on the Ballot

Death of a Suitor

A Dash of Murder

Death at a Diner

A Myrtle Clover Christmas (late 2022)

Southern Quilting Mysteries in Order:

Quilt or Innocence

Knot What it Seams

Quilt Trip
Shear Trouble
Tying the Knot
Patch of Trouble
Fall to Pieces
Rest in Pieces
On Pins and Needles
Fit to be Tied
Embroidering the Truth
Knot a Clue
Quilt-Ridden
Needled to Death
A Notion to Murder
Crosspatch (late 2022)

The Village Library Mysteries in Order (Debuting 2019):
Checked Out
Overdue
Borrowed Time
Hush-Hush
Where There's a Will
Frictional Characters
Spine Tingling
A Novel Idea

Memphis Barbeque Mysteries in Order (Written as Riley Adams):
Delicious and Suspicious
Finger Lickin' Dead
Hickory Smoked Homicide

Rubbed Out

And a standalone "cozy zombie" novel: Race to Refuge, written as Liz Craig